Call Me Juan

By Robert Torres

Call Me Juan

Robert Torres, MA
RT Publishing
Bakersfield, California

Printed in the United States of America

ISBN: 978-0-9903673-0-7

Introduction

The following story is based on an actual incident. The characters of the story are mostly manufactured, although some of them are based on real life figures of the period. The circumstances of the story, however, are factual.

In 1933 an estimated 25,000 destitute migrant workers, mostly of Mexican heritage, set in motion one of America's greatest agricultural strikes. Abandoned by mainstream labor organizations, the workers accepted the leadership of the Cannery and Agriculture Workers Industrial Union. The union's alleged communist affiliation sparked a tremendous backlash from conservative groups throughout California.

The San Joaquin Valley farming machine used propaganda, physical intimidation, and their political influence with the local legal systems to brutally break the back of the five-county strike.

During the three week confrontation, many workers were beaten; several raids occurred on union meetings, and the courts and jails were clogged with illegally detained union members. The intensity of the violence gained international attention when the Mexican Government intervened on behalf of the Mexican nationals who were among those being denied basic civil and human rights.

In response, the United States Government threatened the use of military force until California Governor John Rolf sent in a legion of state police and a team of mediators to end the strike.

Painted on a backdrop of racism, local public opinion generally supported the efforts of the farm owners and their henchmen who perpetrated many criminal acts. In the end, those who committed these crimes were never held accountable.

Chapter One

Jake Rogers awoke to the hum of his house fan. He did not know what time it was, but from the angle of the sun beating down through the window to the foot of his bed, he guessed it was mid-morning.

Despite the action of the fan, the heat of the day was already unbearable, and Jake lay in sweat soaked sheets. There is only one way to describe September temperatures in the San Joaquin Valley: hot.

Jake struggled to focus on the noises coming from the street. The activity level seemed unusually high for a Sunday, but it was hard to say because he found he could not concentrate on the sounds enough to make them out. A tequila hangover can be brutal.

Swinging his legs over the side of his bed, Jake sat in a stupor, his head throbbing. He sat there for several minutes, wondering to himself if there was anything in the house to eat. He decided to brew some coffee. Breakfast could wait.

He shuffled across the two room apartment in his underwear to the kitchen area, where he turned on the hot-plate and grabbed his coffeepot. Coffee brewing, he wandered over to the window to look at the new day, and to see what was happening on Main Street.

He had been right. There was an unusual amount of activity. The migrant workers arriving for the fall cotton harvest were coming in a little early this year. Without screens on the windows Jake could lean out and get a good view of the main drag from the second story of his wood framed dwelling.

The dusty road that served the heart of the community was lined with weather beaten buildings, made up of small stores, an eating establishment, and a couple of taverns. Telephone poles seemed to separate the buildings, and in the distance he could see the steeple of the First Baptist Church, where the community elite met on Sundays to reinforce social ties.

His head pounded as he leaned out to see what was going on, and he felt faint for a second. He closed his eyes and regrouped, and took another look at the center of town. Either it was the run-down appearance of the town, or the hangover, he wasn't sure which, that affected his attitude this morning. But he was in a lousy mood.

"I've got to get out of this place," he

thought to himself.

Citrus Grove had never felt like home, but he had nowhere else to go. There was a depression on, and he was doing okay. Now was probably not the best time to make a move. Besides, why jeopardize what little he had. Too many people were struggling just to survive. He could wait until times were better. At least he was getting by for now.

Citrus Grove was an old farming town. It had originally sprouted up along the railroad right-of-way when the Southern Pacific built its line down the Valley from Sacramento almost a half century earlier.

The town had been named after the first crop to grow in the area. Orange trees had been imported in by the first migrants, who settled on property that had been purchased from the Southern Pacific. Local historians believe the first settlers were probably German, although no one knows for sure.

As the story goes, Citrus Grove was a shadow community. Small towns that refused to pay kickbacks to corrupt railroad owners were bypassed by the railroad. The rail lines were still close by, but the railroad built their own stations, and these shadow towns sprung up around the railroad owned depots. To punish those towns that wouldn't knuckle under, the railroads would bypass them. Even if they built their own stations, the Southern Pacific built their tracks as far as miles from these uncooperative communities.

These so-called shadow towns--or spite towns as the locals called them--were communities that were established and supported by the railroad as a way of marginalizing those communities that would not play the railroad game. The railroad companies would build a station several miles from an existing town where a community would grow and compete with the original towns. Without access to the transportation that the railroads offered, farmers could not get their products to market. Many of the original communities were ultimately reduced to ghost towns, which, of course, was the goal of the railroad owners.

Jake heard the top to his coffeepot rattling in the background. The coffee was ready. After pouring his morning transfusion of caffeine, he sat down and surveyed his shabby little apartment while he sipped the bitter liquid. He went to the cupboard to retrieve some sugar, but he was out of cream, so he would have to drink his coffee black this morning.

"Coffee without cream. How uncivilized," Jake Thought.

He surveyed his surroundings as he sipped his coffee. The paint was peeling in spots off the plastered walls while cheap rugs scattered around the room hid the stained wood floors. There were no curtains on the windows.

He hadn't much to show for his life. Still, he was better off than many. And although he would not be considered very well to-do by community standards, having a sound roof over his head, enough to eat and a little beer money in his pocket, he was living pretty high, compared to his childhood.

Every time Jake pondered this, concerns over his current standard of living disappeared as an issue. Things could be a lot worse. Growing up a poor kid, he was thankful for the least little thing. And he was constantly amazed at how many people he met seemed to complain about their lives while at the same time having so much more than he had ever hoped for. Life was strange.

He dressed slowly and refilled his cup before heading for the door to the outside stairs that led down the back of the building.

He reached for the door knob and twisted, but he had to yank at it a couple of times before it would open. Moisture had warped the jam over time.

He descended the stairs and entered the back door to the shop below his apartment, where he published the town's only newspaper, the Citrus Grove Lantern.

The Lantern was a small weekly publication that survived off of local advertising. The paper wasn't big enough for county interest because of its small and localized circulation. About the only advertising revenue Jake could expect was from the farmers and merchants of the town.

But it was a living, and for now it would have to do. Sipping his coffee and rummaging through some of his notes, Jake considered getting some work done but decided against it temporarily in favor of breakfast.

Just as Jake exited the front door to his shop, he heard some yelling across the street. Turning, he noticed that the commotion seemed to be centered on John Osgood, son of J.C. Osgood, the biggest farmer in the County, and the most respected, or perhaps feared, man in town.

John Jr., or J-J, which is what Bobby

Jones and Bill Fredericks called him, probably the only two friends he had in the world, stood spread-legged on the boardwalk in front of two Mexican farm workers who had the misfortune to run into the arrogant and obnoxious trio.

The workers had just stepped out of the general store, arms laden with groceries, when the older of the two accidentally bumped into Osgood, a serious mistake for a new comer to Citrus Grove.

"Yeah, I'm talking' to you," John Jr. yelled with unmistakable sarcasm. "Can't you understand English?"

He knew that the workers probably could not understand. But he was amusing himself and his friends at the expense of the unlucky newcomers. John Jr. was six-foot-two without his boots, and he weighed about 220 pounds. He was probably ten inches taller and 75 pounds heavier than the by-now thoroughly intimidated young man who was trying to stand his ground in the face of possible disaster.

Mexican farm workers learned quickly in Citrus Grove to step around local residents. Even those who considered themselves enlightened when it came to race relations had little patience for the outsiders. However, without those outsiders to do the donkey work, the town would dry up and blow away.

Farmers needed the seasonal labor, and the merchants made a killing by inflating prices during the harvest season. Profits from the months of September and October were nearly enough to carry most of the merchants through to the next season. Local trade filled in the gaps but was not enough to support the town the year around.

In late summer locals knew enough to stock up on necessary goods in anticipation of the changing fall economy. In this way they could avoid the higher prices. But of course, they could always get the "local price" if nobody was looking. Many of the merchants in town had a delivery service for locals with a cash-on-delivery method of payment. In this way, merchants could maintain a two-price system, giving full-time residents a better deal.

Other merchants offered credit to locals, which meant that the purchases would simply be logged for later payment at a local rate. This way the farm workers could be gouged without making it seam they were being taken advantage of. Not only did farmers get their crops picked, the area businessmen made a tidy profit to boot.

As abusive as this system was, Jake

knew of other communities in the Valley that simply segregated their stores. In many Valley towns Mexicans could not purchase anything on the white side of town.

Jake knew of merchants in other areas that displayed signs in their front windows that read, "No Mexicans, dogs or Niggers allowed." At least it did not go that far in Citrus Grove; so the residents considered themselves enlightened. Jake was not so sure.

Jake knew that the culture of the young man standing on the boardwalk in front of J-J would prevent him from making a choice that would result in loss of face. Mexicans were proud people, and even though the difference in size made a physical confrontation ridiculous, Jake knew that if the young man could not find a respectable way out, he might do something stupid.

Loss of face in Mexican culture under these circumstances translated into a question of one's manhood. It was unthinkable to be humiliated in public without standing up for one's self. Even boys were anxious to seek the respect that went with the recognition that one had attained manhood, which is what made this situation so dangerous.

Jake ambled across and down the street

toward the rising commotion. A good newspaper man is always looking for a story, and John Jr. was good for a little blurb at least once a month.

J-J's father chastised Jake every time his son's activities made the local news, but most of what John Jr. did was benign enough, usually just a lot of drinking and bone-headedness. Except that time last year when the drunken John Jr. nearly beat a man to death for looking at his girlfriend. At least J.J. thought of her in that way. But it was mostly imaginary.

She was like the other girls in town. J.J.'s family money made him attractive, although he was not hard to look at, but all the girls in town knew that getting involved with him was a scary proposition. He had a mean disposition on his good days, and he drank a lot, a lethal combination. Parents typically shuddered at the thought of their daughters marrying J.J. because of his reputation.

John senior had to call in several markers from both the sheriff's office and the district attorney to get John Jr. out of that one. Fortunately for everyone involved, the man survived. However, he left town soon after his recovery.

Then, of course, there was that little

incident a couple of years ago when John Jr. set fire to his neighbor's barn. The neighbor had the poor judgment to tell J-J's father about the cow his son tortured and killed just to watch it die. John Sr. paid for the cow and the barn, and the incident was swept under the rug by local authorities.

The man had decided not to press charges, although the fact that John Sr. was the major stockholder of the bank that held the man's mortgage helped that along a little. And obtaining the cooperation of the district attorney in getting the charges dropped was easy enough, since John Sr. was president of the Tulare County Farmers Association, and without the farmers' financial backing, Robert Green probably could not have gotten re-elected district attorney.

John Jr.'s ability to stay out of serious legal trouble also rested on the fact that because local residents knew he was capable of just about anything, they usually gave him a wide path. He had very little opposition from locals.

As to the current situation, the young farm worker did not know who John Jr. was, and the young man, seemingly in his mid-teens, was about to get his teeth knocked out if someone did not get J.J. under control.

Jake moved closer, and by now John Jr. had shoved the worker around to the point that groceries were strewn in several directions. As a result, the young man out of frustration made the mistake of taking a swing at his oppressor, which is what J-J had undoubtedly been after from the beginning.

He hit the young man, who could not have been more than sixteen, and the youth crashed into the street like he had been thrown from the back of a horse. He lay motionless, his eyes glazed over as he lay flat on his back, his arms spread wide. It seldom took more than one of J.J.'s punches to put someone out. His ham-hock hands were hardened from years of farm work.

John Jr. casually descended the boardwalk steps and sauntered over to where the boy lay. He reached down and grabbed the young man's shirt, effortlessly jerked him to nearly a standing position as if he was a rag doll, and drew back to hit him again when Jake stepped up from behind and intervened.

"He'll never feel it," Jake commented matter of fact. "If you hit him again, you may kill him."

John Jr. glanced around at Jake and

turned loose of the young man's shirt, letting him slump back to the ground. The boy was coming around, but he still didn't know where he was.

"You always did have a soft spot for these goddamn greasers," John Jr. said. "Why don't you just mind your own damn business?"

"You wouldn't want me to tell your daddy you're being a bad boy again, would you Johnny boy?" Jake responded with obvious sarcasm. "If I remember right, he told you about a hundred times to stay out of trouble. He might take your toys away from you. Or, he might not let you hang around with your hoodlum friends anymore."

Jake did not have a reputation for being a town brawler like John Jr., but he was six feet tall and an in-shape 195 pounds. And, he had clearly shown over time that he was not afraid of John Jr., unlike many of the other men in town.

J-J was the typical bully. He tended to pick on only those who he knew would not fight back, or who he knew he could whip, which, due to his size, probably amounted to most of the men in town. But, also due to his size and reputation, he seldom had to prove himself the better man.

The fact that J-J did not have many battles probably worked in Jake's favor, since in reality J-J had little experience street fighting. Not that Jake had much more, but he knew that a big man's size can be used against him by someone who is smarter. And if Jake knew anything, he knew that J-J was an imbecile. His arrogance was his biggest shortcoming. The fact that he believed nobody in town could whip him, or would even try, might cause him to be careless if he met up with a determined and able foe, a theory Jake hoped he would never have to test.

Jake's 32 years to John Jr.'s 23 years also seemed to help. Jake was a little older and more sure of himself. He had spent years maneuvering his way around the so-called upper crust of town.

He was comfortable in all settings, and because of his position in the community, he knew everyone of importance in Citrus Grove, in the entire county for that matter. And, he was clearly not afraid of John Jr. like the typical 18 to 20-year-olds the bully was used to picking on.

Jake's position as newspaper editor also offered him a measure of shelter from John Jr.'s wrath. Not that Jake hid behind his position, but John Jr. was just barely smart enough to understand that Jake could make it tough on him.

Too much adverse public attention to the behavior of an out-of-control son could undermine John Sr.'s position among the farmers. The name John Osgood was becoming recognized state-wide.

Political office at the state level was not out of the question, and the last thing he needed was his son to go around terrorizing potential voters. If he did not have the strength and influence to keep his own kid in line, of what use would he be in the state legislature, or even the governor's office?

John Jr. stood erect and gave Jake a look that could only be described as hatred.

"You can't hide behind that newspaper forever," John Jr. said. "Some day you'll get yours."

"Maybe so. But for now, why don't you leave that young man alone and go about your business."

John Jr. laughed loudly for the benefit of his friends and the crowd that had by now gathered. He proved himself to be the best man, or so he convinced himself. But the laugh was strained. He had been shown up in public again by Jake. J-J was a thug, and everyone in town knew it.

But it was only Jake who had the guts to confront him on a crowded Main Street on a bright and sunny Sunday morning without fear of retribution. J-J would not forget this slight.

"I guess he knows his place by now anyway," J-J said referring to the boy lying in the street. And he walked away with his friends following behind like heel hounds.

Jake turned back to see if he could help the boy, but a woman had appeared out of nowhere to comfort him. Jake looked at her, startled at her beauty. He stood staring at her for a few seconds. But when she caught his stare, he became embarrassed and walked away.

"It was time for breakfast," he thought.

He needed to get something into his stomach. Maybe some of the queasiness would subside.

Jake knew he could do nothing that the young woman could not do. Besides, the boy was probably all right. It appeared he was already coming around as the woman nursed him back to consciousness. The punch had been wild and not completely on the mark, a point which Jake noted. John Jr. did not move well when excited.

Jake walked two blocks and turned into the "Country Diner," where he had breakfast six out of seven days of the week. As a bachelor, he had little use for cooking his own meals, and he did so only out of desperation.

He was welcomed as usual by Barney Pruitt, the pudgy little cook who owned the restaurant. Barney boasted that he "specialized" in country cooking, and that breakfast was his best meal.

Most people knew, however, that Barney liked to tip the bottle more than most, and usually was too drunk to cook a decent dinner. Consequently, he closed early about every other day, because, he said, that business usually dropped of after lunch.

Jake took his usual seat in the corner booth looking out the front window of the establishment. He liked to be ready if anything happened in town, and made an attempt to be where the action was at all times.

One of the down sides of being a newspaperman for a one-horse publication was that you never were really off duty. There was no such thing as vacation, even if Jake could afford one, and even if he had a place to go. So the news business was his life. He was literally on call for breaking news events 24 hours a day.

Of course, not much happened of any real consequence in Citrus Grove. Things picked up a little during the harvest season; hard work and hard play usually came with the seasonal workers. And that frequently meant trouble.

Barney stood in his greasy apron behind the counter wiping some glasses as Jake entered. He didn't bother to come over to the table like he would have done for most people. Jake was a regular, and Barney simply called out, "Coffee?"

"Yeah, and lots of it," Jake answered. "I'm not at my best today."

"Tough day already?" Barney asked as he poured the black liquid.

"Not really. I just had too much fun last night, and I'm paying the price this morning. I turned to beer several years ago, and when I hit the hard stuff these days, I really suffer," Jake said. "Maybe it's time for me to grow up."

Barney waddled across the wooden floor and handed Jake a large mug of coffee. Jake sat staring out the window to the street, as was his usual habit. Taking the cup from Barney, he began to pour milk into his morning brew.

"Thanks. How about some scrambled eggs and toast? I think that's all I'll have today."

"Coming right up," Barney replied as he headed toward the kitchen.

Jake nursed the coffee while he considered the morning's events. He thought back to the girl who had helped the boy lying in the street. Her beauty had definitely left an impression on him.

He had not thought about it at the time, but he figured her to be in her mid-twenties. She had not acknowledged Jake's presence, other than a casual glance. Instead she devoted her attention to the young man lying on the ground.

Jake did not chase local girls like most of the other bachelors. The town was small, and people talked. He thought back to Geena, who he had met in Gunderson while covering a story at the County Court. He struck up a relationship with her and traveled the 25 miles or so once or twice a week to see her. He had never really taken her seriously, however. She was rich, and he knew her parents did not like him. He knew they would never have approved of anything permanent between him and their daughter. He was simply not of their class. But it was fun while it lasted.

Nobody in town knew about his past, but he had a reputation of frequenting the "lower" side of town, and in a small community, that was enough to separate him from the "proper" people. Even though Jake's business caused him to rub elbows with the upper crust, he was not one of them, and would never be accepted into their ranks.

Of course, his business placed him in many situations that might be considered unsavory by the community elite. If he was to do his job properly, he had no choice but to involve himself in some unsavory situations.

Take that story he did on the new jail built a few years ago in the next county. A prisoner had died, and there was some suggestion that a couple of guards were responsible for the death.

An investigation had been conducted by the State Department of Prisons, but no action had been taken. Jake implied that race might have been part of the scenario, since the guards were white and the prisoner had been Mexican.

The audacity of his implication had resulted in a firestorm of letters to the editor, nearly all of which criticized his reporting. The message was clear from the community leaders:

leave the race issue alone. It was okay to bash the underclass, but don't brush up against the big shots. That was forbidden territory.

"I wonder what Geena is doing these days?" he thought to himself.

Jake snapped back to the present as an old friend entered the restaurant. Deputy Sheriff Gordy Wilcock came in and sat down in the booth across from Jake. Gordy was probably Jake's best friend, although he preferred to keep to himself. But Gordy was a pleasant and outgoing person, and Jake frequently came into contact with law enforcement during his pursuit of stories.

"Well, let's hear it," the deputy said. "What was he into this time?"

"Look, Gordy. Maybe it's best if we just forget this one. It's tough enough on these Mexican workers. If that's the worst that happens to that kid in his lifetime, he'll be lucky," Jake said. "I'm not going to write about the incident in the newspaper. So, you can forget it and you won't look bad. If I print it, the farm workers will be labeled troublemakers even before the harvest begins, and they don't need the bad press."

"It's not like I don't want to do something about it." Gordy said. "It's just that if you print a story, I'll be forced to deal with it, and his dad will put the squeeze on my boss, and it will come down to me. You understand. Don't you?"

"Gordy, I've been in this town long enough to know who pulls the strings around here. I said I wasn't going to print, and I won't."

"Just between us then, what the hell happened?" Gordy asked.

"John Jr. was up to his old tricks," Jake said. "You know how he gets during harvest. It's like open season on these migrant workers. He just can't seem to leave them alone. It's like the winter duck migration to hunters. It's in his blood to be on the hunt.

"I'll tell you what, though, the look in John Jr.'s eyes when he was about to finish that kid off was somehow different this time. That menace is going to go too far someday, and I hope he gets nailed to a cross when he does. This could be a busy season for you."

"I wouldn't be surprised," Gordy said. "With this depression going on everybody is feeling the pressure. It's too bad we have to put up with them Mexicans every year. They're nothing but trouble. Our jail cells start filling up the week before the picking starts and stay full until two weeks after the picking is over. They should stay where they belong."

"The problem," Jake answered, "is that if they did not come here every year to pick the crops the town would fold up and both our jobs would too. Besides, nobody wants them. Many of them don't belong anywhere. Their own country can't provide for them. Most of them are uneducated, and they are unable to establish themselves in any community because they are hated everywhere they go. That is why they are forced to do what they do."

"Why do you always stick up for them?" Gordy asked. "You know they are nothing but trouble."

Barney stepped up with Jake's breakfast and a coffeepot.

"Here you go Jake, coffee Gordy?"

"No. I have to get back to work. See ya, Jake...Barney."

Gordy walked out the front door of the restaurant, and Jake watched out the window as he headed down the street to the sheriff's substation office.

Jake ate his breakfast slowly as several other patrons filtered into the diner. The background conversation picked up as Barney went about his usual business. Jake began to daydream again about the girl on the street.

"I wonder if I will see her again?" he thought.

Citrus Grove, a town of maybe 1000 year-round residents, and about the same living on the outskirts, saw as many as several thousand new faces during the course of the six week cotton harvest. Migrant workers filled the extra housing in the area each fall, crowding as many as several families into a small house.

Many simply parked along the roadsides, virtually living in their dilapidated automobiles and trucks, those who could afford them. If they were lucky, they might gain access to the barracks housing some of the farmers provided to seasonal workers. Even then, the living standards were deplorable. Jake had heard farmers joke that they wouldn't house livestock in some of the places Mexican workers were forced to live.

Farmer housing seldom had running water, electricity or indoor bathrooms. Sometimes the cracks in the walls were so wide the dust filtering in during a wind storm left a layer of filth over everything. And yet, for some of the workers, this was a step up from where they came.

Jake knew the whole California Central Valley would be filled with thousands of workers in the next few weeks. The chance he would see that girl again was very small indeed. Still, his thoughts were filled with her black, wavy hair and her buxom figure. He could not remember ever being so taken with a woman upon such a simple meeting. And they had not even met, not really.

"Maybe I'll see her again," he thought. "Hell, I don't even know her name."

Jake sat staring out the window as he nibbled at his breakfast, half-heartedly consuming the greasy eggs that were Barney's stock in trade. Most people in town who visited the downtown diner criticized the food, but sometimes there is no accounting for the factors that lead to popularity.

Quality is not the only factor that attracts people.

Part of the attraction of the Country Diner was the fact that the best eating establishment in town was a fairly high priced steak house that was not open for breakfast.

Another part of Barney's popularity was tradition; the diner had been there as long as anyone could remember. And most of the long time clientele remember when Barney was a first-rate cook -- before he took to the bottle.

The only other diner in the area was on

the outskirts of town, and not in the center of city activity like Barney's. There was a third in the Mexican side of town, but nobody from the "right" side of the tracks would be caught dead down there.

Jake may have been the only "respectable" person in town who could get away with frequenting the out-of-the-way places, but it was recognized that his job as newspaperman excused him from maintaining the acceptable level of social propriety. Besides, many of his uptown readers forgave his social indiscretions, since they enjoyed reading about the problems on the "lower side of town."

It was a past-time of local residents to sit around Barney's during the dinner hour and remark about the people who lived there. From Jake's point of view, it was almost a necessity to spend time in the lower side of town, since his readers frequently criticized him if he printed anything negative about the "uptown" area.

His livelihood depended on the paper's circulation, which attracted the advertising money needed to support his business. Without that support, Jake would have to pack up and leave Citrus Grove, since he had no other way of making a living.

He had not cultivated the kind of close relationships with mainstream residents that someone else in his position might have done. Jake discovered early that truth was the first casualty in a small town when it came to economic survival. And he resented having to cater to the snobbish tastes of the people who supported him. But he drew the line when it came to socializing with them, not that he would be accepted.

The people in town with money to spend for a newspaper would only support one that promoted a certain point of view. Stories about successful social activities sponsored by prominent, local organizations were acceptable news articles. But when it came to what locals might term "colorful" stories, as far as the movers and shakers in town were concerned, let that kind of thing remain in the Mexican side of town.

What Jake did not confide to his uptown friends is that he actually preferred the people on the other side of the tracks. To him, they were genuine and unpretentious, which was a refreshing contrast to the self-centered elite of the community, who seemed to go out of the way to out-do each other.

In fact, it grated on Jake that he was

simply a tool of the establishment, but he had caved in to the situation long ago. He had been over this in his mind many, many times. Why rock the boat? What would be the point of driving oneself to the poor house? Who really cared, anyway?

"More coffee?" Barney asked.

"Huh? Oh. No thanks. I think I'll go home and try to take a nap," Jake said as he was jolted out of his daydream. "I still haven't recovered from last night."

Barney began clearing away the dirty dishes as Jake dug some money out of his wallet. Placing the proper amount on the table, Jake moved toward the door.

"Thanks, Barney. Probably see you tomorrow."

Sundays were usually quiet around Citrus Grove, although this picking season was going to be different, unknown to Jake as he wandered back toward his apartment, taking in the marginal activity in downtown along the way.

"Damn, it was hot," Jake thought.

Chapter Two

Monday mornings began early for Jake Rogers. Monday through Thursday was the end of Jake's news cycle. This was the period that he was at his busiest. With a Friday noon deadline at the printers in Gunderson -- 25 miles away -- he had to get moving. The driver that took the copy to the printers was very early on Friday mornings to pick up Jake's work.

Mondays and Tuesdays were usually devoted to writing and organizing the week's news. His first stop would be the police station, where Jake went over the weekend's arrest reports. The Friday and Saturday night police records occasionally contained some juicy tidbit that set the community buzzing, so Monday morning was the best day to find out what was going on.

The police log this week seemed pretty routine. At 11:10 Friday night Floyd Henderson was tossed in jail for being drunk again. At 7:30 Saturday night Ricardo Sanchez was arrested for starting a brawl in the Mexican part of town. The police had to respond to a call of domestic abuse Saturday night at 8:45 at the

Broderick residence again. It seemed like a normal weekend.

Jake usually devoted his Wednesdays to the gathering of political news. The first Wednesday of the month, for instance, Jake attended the county Planning Commission meeting in Gunderson, the County seat.

The Citrus Grove City Council met every second and fourth Wednesday of the month. Nothing much occurred at these meetings, and he was able to get a copy of the minutes to each meeting from the City Clerk the following morning.

From the minutes he could report everything that happened if he chose, and Thursday mornings he could always interview the Mayor or councilmen on the issues that were raised at the meetings. So Jake didn't really have to attend the meetings if there was something better to do. But Jake liked to make an appearance at the meetings. It gave him a chance to demonstrate his community spirit. He felt it was good for business.

The same pattern could occur for the Planning Commission or other political functions. This was one of the advantages of a weekly newspaper. There was more time to gather information. The daily newspapers in the area had the advantage of timeliness, but Jake could go into a little more depth on the stories and the impact the news had on the public.

Thursdays usually were spent wrapping things up, unless something unusual happened, such as a robbery or fire. Then he felt obligated to get photos if possible. The paper came out on Friday in the late afternoon, just in time for the weekend grocery ads. This is when Jake could count on hearing public reaction to the week's stories. Usually it was positive, since he seldom broke the social rules.

If Jake got a day off, it was usually on Fridays after he sent his flats to the printer. But on Friday, Saturday and Sunday he liked to circulate around town. The weekend was the prime news period for public events such as parades, local school sports and social activities.

By Monday he had to begin putting everything together. If it wasn't for Sally Conway, his young assistant, who helped with advertising, production and over-the-counter business at his shop, Jake probably would not be in business. He simply could not find enough time, or enthusiasm, to do it all for himself.

This Monday was much like all the rest. Sally worked on the obituaries, wedding announcements and classifieds, while Jake reviewed this week's City Council agenda.

When there was time, Jake spent Monday afternoons, and occasionally Tuesday mornings, at the sheriff's office, gathering last minute arrest information from the police log, which is where he became acquainted with his friend Gordy.

If there was something special going on at the County Court in Gunderson that week, Jake might take his flats to the printer himself, and if there was a last minute news item, he could be found at the Gunderson Globe, the county newspaper, working on last minute changes.

The Globe provided Jake with a place to work on late stories. After all, he wasn't competing with them, and he occasionally could help them out in return if something hot hit Citrus Grove. It was a very cozy situation for Jake.

He had considered in the past going to work for the Globe, and maybe that could be his bail out if things didn't work out in Citrus Grove. But he would be giving up a lot of independence. And, besides, he didn't have to work very hard, even though he didn't make much money.

There was little spare time for a small

town newspaperman, however. He practically lived his life around his work.

As usual Jake was thoroughly absorbed in what he was doing. The deadlines loomed. And the printer wasn't very sympathetic in the event a printing customer was late. He had made deadline commitments to other customers, so Jake knew if he was late it was likely that the printer would set up for another job and Jake's newspaper would not be printed on time.

A late newspaper had a domino effect. Grocery ads for instance, targeted for weekend trade, would not get their maximum exposure. It was essential for Jake to keep a good relationship with his advertisers.

The small bell attached to the front door to announce the entrance of a customer, usually wanting to purchase classified space, sounded its distinctive tinkle. As was his habit, Jake ignored the sound, preferring to keep his typewriter going and knowing that Sally would handle the counter. It was the voice that caught his attention.

"May I speak to Jake Rogers," she asked.

He looked up; it was her!

"I'm Jake," he said over Sally's shoulder from the back of the shop.

"How can I help you?"

He felt butterflies as he rose from his desk and walked over to the counter. For the first time he really looked at the young woman who had dominated his thoughts for the last 24 hours. She was even more attractive than he remembered. She had very dark hair and an olive complexion. At about five feet two, she had to look up to Jake as he stood across the counter.

His first serious glance fell to her ring finger.

"No wedding ring," he thought.

"My name is Veronica Camacho," she said. "You helped one of our workers yesterday, and I came to thank you."

Jake tried to act nonchalant, but he began to sweat from his nervousness. He could not believe that she had just walked into his shop, and he wanted to make sure she did not get away before he got some information about her. He wanted to be able to see her again.

"It was nothing," he said. "I just didn't want to see the young man get hurt. Have you been in town long?"

"Oh, we arrived a couple of days ago. This is my third season here in the valley, but it's Ricardo's first time, and he hasn't learned yet how to stay out of trouble."

"Is that his name?" Jake asked to keep the conversation flowing.

"Yes, Ricardo Castañon. "He hasn't worked in the United States before, and he doesn't know what he is dealing with."

"It wouldn't make any difference if he did with John Jr. around."

"Who?"

"The man who hit your friend," Jake said. "You people really need to know who to stay away from…"

She seemed to cringe a little at his "you people" remark, and he immediately regretted it. He had never considered himself a ladies man, and he just could not seem to get the hang of how to say the right thing. Nevertheless, Veronica seemed to take the remark in stride.

"I had another reason for coming," she said. "I want to purchase some space in your newspaper. We are having a union rally outside of town this Saturday, and I want to get the word out."

Once Jake had moved to the counter, Sally had gone back to her desk in order to resume her other business. But she caught the remark about the union and refocused her attention on the young woman at the counter.

"A union rally?" Jake asked in his best newspaperman's tone. "I don't think we have ever had a union around here. Which union are you talking about?"

"It's the Cannery and Agricultural Workers Industrial Union, the CAWIU. It's a fairly new organization from San Jose, but we have been active throughout the valley this season."

"Is that the same union that led the Taugus Ranch strike earlier this year?" Jake asked, now riveting his attention on what she was saying instead of her appearance.

"Yes, that is the one."

Sally was by now giving the young woman her undivided attention. She had been in the news business just long enough to see a chance of a real story developing, and she also knew the possible problems a union could cause.

"That strike was pretty messy," Jake remarked. "Are you planning a strike here in Citrus Grove?"

His news nose was beginning to show, and Veronica began to back-peddle somewhat.

"We are just holding a rally in order to pass out information," she said. "I assume we can count on our local newspaper to be represented at the rally."

Jake thought he saw the opening he was hoping for and went with it.

"It's my job, of course, to report on news events in town. When and where is it going to be held?"

"I have written up what I want to say," she said. "I was hoping you would help me with spelling. And if you will tell me how much I owe you, I will pay and be on my way."

"Sally will help you with that," Jake said as he moved away with the paper she had given him.

He kicked himself about that "you-people" crack he made. Had he alienated her before he even had a chance to get to know her? He decided to step back and let things lay for now, before he said something else stupid. He expected to see her at the union rally anyway, where he could make a fresh start.

Veronica paid her bill and left.

"Thanks again for your help yesterday," she said to Jake across the room as she paused at the door.

She left before he could respond, but he felt better that she at least apparently left on an upbeat note. Maybe he had not blown it after all.

The next few days passed quickly. Carloads of migrant workers poured into town, and merchant cash registers sprang to life. The local gas station, sundry and grocery stores all prospered during the harvest, especially the day after paydays.

Citrus Grove was transformed into a bustling community, with the usual problems that went with the subsequent overcrowding. Drinking establishments, the card house and pool hall also experienced a significant increase in activity. It reminded Jake of the stories he had read in school about the boom towns during the Gold Rush. The atmosphere was electric.

This year, however, the atmosphere was markedly different. The news of the union spread like wildfire. Jake received considerable criticism from members of the local farming community for printing the rally announcement. One farmer went as far as to threaten Jake while he was eating at Barney's. A couple of farmers came in while Jake sat in his usual booth and directed some derogatory remarks at him.

"That advertisement for the union rally was a bad idea," said one farmer in bib overalls.

"What were you thinking?"

"I run a newspaper, and that is news. Besides, when people pay for the space, I print it. That is how I stay in business. What is wrong with that?"

"Well, if this thing goes too far," the farmer responded, "people around here will remember you helped get it going. We don't need no unions here. We've got along just fine without them for a long time. The last thing we need in this town is for those mezkins to get organized."

Jake had not been surprised with that attitude, but he did not realize the depth of the sentiment.

Saturday rolled around, and CAWIU banners began to appear at Legion Park in the center of town. Jake arrived shortly after dawn, even though the rally was not supposed to begin until 9 a.m. He wanted to watch the activities as they developed. He noticed that others apparently had the same idea. Many people arrived early. A few helped assemble the platform that someone obviously intended to use to address the expected audience.

Most of the faces were new to Jake, but he recognized several residents from the Mexican part of town. Some of the migrants had returned often enough so that they had established themselves locally and abandoned the migrant ways. They pooled their resources, and some even opened small businesses, which catered primarily to their own people. Whites seldom, if ever, patronized the Mexican establishments.

Jake also noticed that a few farmers showed up, apparently out of curiosity, or possibly out of dread for the expected consequences of a union in town. Or, it may have been that they were simply spying in order to help the other farmers to create a counter strategy. Jake suspected this may have been the case. And, of course, John Jr. and his rat-pack strolled onto the scene minutes before the rally began.

"The vultures are circling," Jake thought.

Jake was amazed at the size of the crowd. Over the next couple of hours, as Jake circulated around the park, there may have been over 100 workers, with more arriving by the minute, who had congregated in the area. The only time Jake had seen this many people at the park was during 4th of July celebrations.

The park was used by the local American Legion to put on the annual Independence Day celebration. They had donated cannon for the park, and on special occasions Legion volunteers fired it to commemorate whatever holiday was being celebrated.

"Well, what do you think?" asked a voice.

Jake turned to see Gordy stepping up beside him.

"I don't know," said Jake. "I have never seen anything like it."

"My boss says there have been several union rallies around the county this week," Gordy said. "He is afraid this could get ugly. Some fist-fights broke out in Farmerville, and strike talk is beginning to grow."

"I can't believe there would be a strike," Jake said. "Times are hard enough with the Depression and all. What would be achieved?"

"I don't know, but this union is gaining a reputation for rabble-rousing. There is word that the Farmers Association is planning a meeting for tomorrow."

"On Sunday?" Jake asked.

"I guess they want to see what becomes of this rally, and then make plans of their own. I am telling you, Jake, we could be in for big trouble. There were hospitalizations during the strike over in Taugus a few months ago."

"I see somebody I know," Jake said suddenly. "I will talk to your later."

He moved quickly through the crowd. He had spotted Veronica as she passed out some flyers near the union platform. Gordy watched from a distance with some interest as Jake and Veronica spoke.

"Hi," Jake said. "We meet again. What have you got there?"

"Some union literature," she said. "Here, take one."

Jake accepted the piece of paper, and he stuck it in his pocket. He was more interested in Veronica for the moment. He would look at the handout later.

"How is your friend?" Jake asked.

"Ricardo? Oh, he is all right. He was sore for a couple of days, but he is young and strong. The physical pain was not as bad as the injured pride. He is carrying hard feelings for the man who hit him."

"Ricardo would be smart to leave John Jr. alone," Jake said. "He is not someone to mess with. He has gotten away with his bullying for so long, people don't even bother to complain anymore. They just stay out of his way."

"Who is this man that he can beat up

on boys without being punished?" Veronica asked. "Is it because we are not white?"

"I'm afraid that is part of it. But in his case, he will pick on anyone who gets in his way. His father owns half of Tulare County."

"Does that give him the right to act like an animal?"

"Unfortunately, I am afraid it does." Jake said. "What is that platform for?"

"Pat Chambers, the CAWIU union organizer from San Jose, is going to speak. We are trying to recruit as many people as possible before we give our demands to the Farmers Association."

"Picking is due to start Monday." Jake said. "When do you expect to give your demands to the Association?"

"Tomorrow," she said. "At their meeting."

"You are very well informed. I only found out this morning that they had intended to meet. How did you know?"

"I didn't," she said. "It's just that it happens the same way everywhere we go. The farmers always plan a meeting once they find out we are having a union rally. We expected it to happen that way. That is part of the reason for the announcement in your paper, to give a message to local farmers of our intentions."

"I guess I underestimated you," Jake said. "I will pay closer attention from now on."

"Oh, I think you paid plenty of attention to me when I was in your office," Veronica said with a coy smile. "But you were paying more attention to my breasts than to your news business."

Jake's face flushed red. It is true he had been appreciating her figure when she stood in front of him at his office, but he did not realize how poorly he disguised it.

"Are you always so outspoken?" he asked.

"Not always, only with people I like. I don't believe in playing games."

Jake was caught off guard. He was pleased and intimidated at the same time. He was used to women who angled their way around men. The straight, up front approach was new to Jake. He liked this woman, more than he could remember liking any woman.

Jake was a little flustered and not sure of what to say next, so he uncomfortably decided to excuse himself.

"Well, I guess I should get back to work," he said. "I hope to see you again."

"We are having a union meeting soon,"

she said. "When we make definite plans, I will let you know and you can come and listen."

"That will be fine," Jake said, and he moved across the street to the steps of the American Legion Building so he could get a better view of the platform over the heads of the growing crowd.

The audience quieted as a soft spoken, smallish man ascended the platform. He began his speech with a general discussion about the place of the workingman, and how local farmers could not exist without the means to harvest their product.

"Where would they be without us?" he asked the crowd. "Would they pick the crops themselves?"

Spectators mumbled and murmured as the man continued.

"The working man has always gotten the short end of the stick," Chambers said in a more forceful voice. "The employer has always had the upper hand. All we want is a fair shake, decent working conditions and a fair day's pay for a fair day's work. Is that too much to ask?"

The crowd response was louder and more enthusiastic this time.

As the man continued, Jake felt more and more uneasy about the direction this was going. The union organizer promised that if the workers joined the CAWIU, their strength of numbers could gain a great return during negotiations with the Farmers Association.

The rally went on for about 20 minutes, not long enough to bore anyone, and not long enough to say everything the man on the platform obviously wanted to say. He seemed well practiced at his trade, and left the crowd with many unanswered questions, like how was the union going to accomplish what it promised about a better future.

Nevertheless, Jake's admiration for Chambers grew. It didn't seem possible that such an outwardly low key individual could bring a crowd to such a fever pitch. As time passed, the spectators became more and more raucous.

Jake did not have much experience with union tactics, but he spotted immediately the tactic that Chambers was using.

Jake knew that Chambers' purpose was to be vague in the beginning. It wouldn't be very smart to put all of one's cards on the table too soon. Not only would it enhance the ability of the opposition to formulate an opposing plan, but it could adversely affect recruitment by scaring off prospective members. There was no need to give the workers too much to think about too soon.

In parting the man left with an invitation to join the fight for a better life. Who was against a better life, especially during these times? It was important to generate enthusiasm at first. The bad news would come later, like how the farmers would fight tooth and nail to resist unionism.

It was also not in the union's best interest to bash the farmers too early. Chambers could have discussed more thoroughly what he meant by a better life, the conditions that workers suffered in the company housing, for example; he refrained.

But stirring up the farm owners too early was also not a good idea. Chambers certainly knew what the farmers were capable of. Veronica had suggested that the union had much experience dealing with them. She even seemed to know how they would react to the union's first salvo.

Yes indeed, Chambers knew this was just the beginning. No need to give the workers too much to think about too early, nor the farmers, for that matter.

It also appeared that the union leaders had planned well in other ways. Jake had noticed the tables in front of the raised platform and wondered why they were there.

At the end of the speech, union leaders moved to the tables to hand out literature and answer questions.

"First things first," Jake thought. "Get their attention and then sign them up while they are in the mood to get involved."

When the men began moving to the tables to sign up, the eggs and tomatoes began to fly.

Jake saw several young men behind the platform as they pitched their fodder into the crowd. Several workers were hit, and they responded by chasing the perpetrators through the park until they were out of sight.

Jake could not possibly know at the time that he was witnessing a glimpse of what was to come.

"See what I mean," Gordy said as he stepped up next to Jake on the American Legion Hall steps. "These union people are nothing but trouble."

"Maybe," Jake said. "But you have to admit that these workers do have it pretty tough. Look at the way they live. I wonder how many of these farmers would be willing to do this work for the wages they pay."

"That kind of talk will get you in trouble, Jake. You had better keep those ideas to yourself around here."

"I guess you're right," Jake said with some irritation. "Excuse me. I have to go back to the office and write it up. I've got a feeling this is going to be a busy week."

Jake returned to his office. Many things were swirling around in his mind, not the least of which was Veronica. He sat down at his desk in the quiet shop and remembered the leaflet she had given him. Taking it out of his pocket, he read it thoroughly.

It contained much of the same kind of rhetoric presented at the rally by Chambers. He thought about the words of the man, and began to question in his mind what the quiet but intense man had said.

It was true, he thought to himself, that migrant workers had a tough life in the valley, but ever since the Stock Market Crash four years ago, many people had it tough. Did the farmers have it any better than the workers?

He thought about that for a while in an attempt to answer his own question.

Of course they did, he concluded. They lived in decent houses. They were supported by the community, which included credit and goods for non-inflated prices at local merchants, as well as relatively unrestricted access to bank loans. Their kids had the opportunity to go to school and live stable lives, with a home to go to every night.

And, now that he thought about it, he had printed several stories in the past year or so about hundreds of thousands of dollars in federal subsidies that had been distributed to farmers throughout the state.

Government programs supported farmers by giving them sizable financial grants. That money could be used to help pay their mortgages, pay their feed bills, and purchase new equipment.

The government went as far as to pay some farmers not to plant certain crops. In other words, some farmers were encouraged to do nothing so they could be paid for it by the government. It actually made economic sense, because when there was less product on the market, the prices stabilized.

Sure, many farmers were going under just like many other kinds of businesses, but it wasn't because the government or local communities had turned their backs on them.

Farmers also had access to cheap water, subsidized by the programs established by the

Department of Agriculture and the Reclamation Act. The Reclamation Act provided federal subsidies to build dams and aqua ducts. It also provided low cost loans to sink water wells.

Did workers have any of this kind of support? Not really. Of course there were food programs around, and some migrant workers had access to those, at least those workers who were in the United States legally. But so did everyone else who was hurting because of the Depression. Farm workers did not enjoy special attention.

For the average farmer, the primary concern was the fluctuating market prices for their goods and what that year's profit margin would be. The average farm worker in 1933 woke up each morning worrying about how to feed their families for another day, not whether or not they were going to make their tractor payment on time that month.

When times got better and the emergency support programs ended for the average person, including migrant workers, the farmers would still enjoy their privileged place in local society and would come out even better than before. But too many of these same farmers, the Mexican workers would still be a just bunch of greasers.

No, Jake thought. The playing field was not level. Workers were definitely at a disadvantage, which is probably why unions began to emerge in the first place. If the farmers were unhappy with the rise of unionism in the valley, they only had themselves to blame. Perhaps if they had treated their workers with more respect from the beginning, it wouldn't have to come to this.

Jake continued to consider these things as he wrote a series of articles about the rally. He continued to work for the rest of the day and into the night.

"Quite a day," he thought as he finally leaned back in his chair.

"This is exciting," he thought, as he made the decision to attend the Farmers Association meeting the next day.

Chapter Three

Tracking down the location of the farmer's meeting was quite easy. If it was a gathering of a few of the prominent men in town, it would usually take place at the ranch house of J.C. Osgood. In the event it was to be a meeting of sizable proportions, it would probably be conducted at the American Legion Hall. And Jake reasoned that quite a few of the local farmers would be in attendance, so he headed for the Hall.

The Mexican community attended their events at what had become known as the Union Hall; although it was in reality a dilapidated old building that had been left vacant after old man Billingsley died and nobody stepped forward to claim the property.

Leading members of the Mexican community had raised the funds to pay the back taxes on the building before the state confiscated it, and they turned it into a public meeting place, where weddings, dances and other social gatherings were held.

Interestingly enough, it was the only building in the white part of town where Mexicans were welcome. White community members were upset about this, but since it was the Mexican community that came to the building's rescue when it looked like the County would take it, they were left alone.

And since it was in the business district, it was tolerated. Even then, the City Council would have managed to pass some kind of local ordinance resulting in the confiscation of the building for city use if it had not been for the sensitivity of the Mexican community.

They decided to only use the building after business hours so as not to offend the white community. By allowing this situation to exist, liberal white members of the community could tout the racial tolerance of Citrus Grove to surrounding towns.

Other than the so-called Union Hall, the park had effectively become the dividing line between the Mexican and white communities, although it was mostly used by local farm workers and their families for picnics and other outdoor activities. Most social events among the white community took place on the private property of one of the community's leading citizens.

The park had been named Legion Park by the City Council in honor of the city's WWI veterans who were members of the local chapter of the American Legion. The irony was that the American Legion was an informal white's only organization, and white people never used the park.

Legion Park was nevertheless one of the most pleasant places in town. Many mature oak trees dotted the park and provided ample shade. Not a weekend from spring through fall would find the park vacant. Many community families picnicked there. There was also a dirt baseball diamond that had been scratched out and maintained. A small river ran nearby, where many of the older men congregated in the guise of fishing. Of course, their real purpose was male bonding out of earshot of the women and a liberal amount of beer consumption. The park was a pleasant place indeed.

Jake meandered over to the park at about 10:00 a.m. The farmers would meet around mid-day, which was their custom. Maybe the farmers saw something dramatic about the idea of meeting at high noon. It seemed to give them an air of self importance.

He decided to go a little early to watch the events as they developed, and going early provided him with the opportunity to visit with his Mexican friends without raising the eyebrows of the so called decent people of the community. Everybody would know why he was there, or at least his presence would seem to have a legitimate purpose because of the circumstances. So he wouldn't have to compromise his standing in the white community by being seeing in the Mexican part of town, not that he cared all that much.

As he wandered around the park lost in his thoughts, Jake noticed the arrival of some old friends. Nicholas and Beatrice Delgado were unpacking some supplies for the noon meal. They enjoyed coming to the park on Sundays, as did many of their friends.

The park attracted many people on weekends and holidays. It was probably the only place in town where friends could gather and discuss the events of the week: which couples had become engaged, family illnesses, the upcoming harvest, who was expecting a new baby, those sort of things.

Jake particularly enjoyed the extended family system of his Mexican friends. Mexican tradition held that grandparents, aunts and uncles, god parents and in-laws alike were all part of the immediate family. There was always room for one more, and Jake was accepted as nearly one of the family.

Jake approached the Delgado's as they

unloaded a table and chairs from their old flatbed truck.

"Hello," Jake greeted his friends. "Nice day."

"Si, esta muy bien," Delgado responded after he recognized who had spoken. "Como esta? We haven't seen much of you lately."

"I've been very busy. You know how it is. How is your son, Jaime?"

"Lo mismo," Delgado answered. "I am afraid he will always be the same."

Jake had met the Delgado's after their teen-aged son had been found beaten senseless and left by the side of an irrigation canal near the edge of town. The boy never fully recovered. He suffered brain damage from a blow to the head, believed to be from a piece of wood.

Nobody was convicted or even charged with the beating, and the boy could not name his assailant. Delgado had his suspicions, but no evidence was ever produced, and the local authorities did not put in much effort investigating the beating of a Mexican kid. The Delgado's were never quite the same. Jaime was their only living child.

Another son had been killed a couple of years earlier in an agricultural accident at a local farm. Child labor was common in the valley, and there were no laws to help workers who were injured on the job.

Nicholas had also been injured while working for an area farmer, and he did not receive any compensation. His right arm was practically useless after it was nearly ripped of by the kick of a backfiring hand crank as he attempted to start a tractor.

He had severely torn one of the bicep muscles in his arm, but he did not have the price of a doctor and had to allow it to heal by itself. His boss refused to help, saying that agriculture was a tough business and workers took their chances. All the workers knew that the tractor was in disrepair, and that it was just a matter of time before someone got hurt.

Delgado had worked his way into a year-round tractor driver position, which is how he managed to escape the migrant life. But, after the accident he was reduced to making a living by picking strawberries and watermelons on the west side of the valley during the early and mid summer harvests, and by picking cotton in the fall.

He was able to supplement his income the rest of the year as a local handyman. He was pretty good with tools and was generally well liked. He couldn't do a lot of heavy lifting, but he was very skilled when it came to fixing things.

Several months had elapsed before his arm had healed enough to return to his tractor position, but by then he had been replaced and there was no job to return to. His employer had felt no loyalty to Delgado. So he lost his job and had been working back in the fields ever since.

It had taken him several years to work his way onto the tractor, and he hoped that he could do it again. But both tractor drivers for his two seasonal employers were younger than Delgado, so getting another shot at advancement would probably mean an injury to one of the other men. And Delgado didn't wish that for anybody.

Beatrice worked as a domestic at the house of one of the local farmers. Between the two, they managed to survive. In the Mexican part of town, property wasn't worth much, so their mortgage payment was low. Nicolas frequently thanked God for that small fact.

Jake had become friends with the Delgados while he investigated their son's beating for the newspaper, and he had remained good friends ever since. Jake respected the quiet dignity of the Delgados as they struggled to maintain their home and family.

Several other people arrived over the next half-hour or so as Jake talked and joked with his friend. Jake also noticed that quite a few farmers had begun to filter into the American Legion Hall across the street, and he begged his leave from the Delgado gathering, saying his good-bys to several of his friends. He then crossed the dirt street in front of the Hall, walked up the steps and entered the building.

As Jake looked around he noticed that about 30 or 40 farmers were already there. More continued to arrive, and they began to pour inside, getting away from the rising heat.

The building had been constructed out of cinder-block, which was an excellent insulator. The building was also only about three years old, and was one of the most modern dwellings in town, built almost entirely out of the donations of the farmers who used it most.

It was called the American Legion Hall, and was outfitted with the obligatory cannon and flagpole in front, but the Legionaries and farmers were essentially one in the same. There were actually a couple of Mexican World

War I veterans in town, but they were not invited to join the local branch of the Legion.

Entrance to the Hall was typically restricted to a chosen few, unless it was being used for a community dance or similar social function. Even then, everyone knew who was welcome and who was not.

Jake saw that J.C. Osgood had arrived and had taken his place center stage in front of the gathering, with several of his lackeys competing for his recognition. Few doubted who the big dog was in Citrus Grove, or in the county for that matter.

Jake stepped up to the group and addressed Osgood in a familiar tone. J.C. Osgood turned to Jake as he approached.

"J.C.," Jake said as a form of greeting. "Can I have a minute of your time?"

"Anything for the press," he answered in a condescending tone, playing it up a little for his entourage. "Excuse me boys."

J.C. Osgood had always been irritated with Jake, because he was one of the few people in town who could not be intimidated or bought. He considered putting Jake out of business more than once for his occasionally unflattering news coverage, but had decided against it. After all, he needed the newspaper more than he disliked Jake.

He could have started his own newspaper, but there was a little more credibility attached to an independent press, and he had made it work for him on a number of occasions, which is what he would attempt to do in this case. As a result, he tolerated Jake and his irreverent attitude.

"And what is the press doing at a simple Farmers Association meeting," Osgood asked Jake, testing his patience. "No fires to report?" he said as a reminder to the way Jake raked John Jr. over the coals after burning down that barn.

"No fires today, no lost dogs or ice cream socials either," Jake responded trying to keep his temper in check and trying to ignore the obvious dig. "But this little farmer get together today could get hot. Everyone knows that the principal purpose of this meeting is to respond to yesterday's union rally."

"What union rally?" Osgood asked in a transparent attempt to throw off the unwelcome newsman. "We are here to set this year's wages. Nothing more."

"Well, what about that union rally in the park yesterday? You're not going to tell me you know nothing about it."

"Oh, I heard about it alright. But it doesn't mean a thing. Other unions have come in here and tried to organize before, but they can't get anywhere.

"These Mexicans can't be organized. They drift around too much. How do you organize people who are too shiftless to stay put long enough to attend union meetings, let alone pay dues. This new union doesn't mean a thing. Excuse me, we are about to start the meeting."

Jake moved toward the back of the room and took a seat. The building had about two hundred farmers inside by now, and seating space was disappearing fast.

Jake detected nothing but confidence in Osgood's voice. He was right when he said that other unions had attempted to organize the migrant workers. The American Federation of Labor tried it many years earlier, but they gave up when the workers could not afford to pay the dues. At least that was the stated reason the union used to abandon the cause.

Jake suspected that race had played a role in the decision. The official AFL explanation was exactly what Osgood had said, that migrant workers could not be organized because of their lifestyle, moving from place to place. Jake was convinced, however, that if the workers were white, the AFL would have tried harder.

He came to that conclusion after the Industrial Workers of the World, also known as the IWW, or Wobblies for short, succeeded where the AFL had failed. The IWW used a colorblind approach to organization, and did quite well at times.

Some of California's most notorious strikes were spearheaded by the IWW, like the one in Northern California in 1917. Jake had read quite a bit about the IWW from old newspaper clippings when he had nothing much else to do.

The Wheatland Riot of 1917, which centered on the Durst Ranch, resulted in the deaths of at least three people, including one deputy sheriff and a local assistant district attorney.

The riot began over several problems. Durst had sent out a recruitment call for 5,000 workers, and people responded from as far away as Texas. The problem was that he had jobs for only about 1,000 or so. Over recruiting was a typical tactic; the goal was to depress the wages by increasing the desperation of those who sought employment.

Most of the people who came for those jobs could not afford to return. For many, it was work or be stranded. Many of them were working paycheck to paycheck, which Jake knew to still be true.

Durst was also accused of not providing water for his workers so his cousin could sell lemonade for a nickel a glass. Witnesses said the so-called lemonade was nothing more than lemon skin dipped into warm water. And a nickel a glass was about five times what it was worth.

On top of that, Durst provided tents to some of his workers to live in, but then deducted a rental fee for those tents from the workers' paychecks.

To make matters even worse, Durst had built one outhouse for the entire crew, and anyone who wanted to use it sometimes had to walk a quarter mile or more to get there, only to find that it had not been cleaned for days. The odor was overpowering, particularly in 100 degree weather.

The workers nearly lynched Durst's foreman when he told them to quit complaining and to get back to work. Durst called in the police, and the riot was on. Since the IWW was on the scene, they got the blame for starting the riot, and several of the union leaders were jailed.

The union was on the right side. The problem, however, was that farmers accused the IWW of socialist affiliation, which kept them afoul of the law, and they could not gain the popular support necessary for any labor movement to succeed.

Labor historians tended to agree that by the 1920s the IWW suffered from the Red Scare that emerged after World War I. When Russia turned to Communism during the Bolshevik Revolution and threatened the world with a communist takeover, many conservatives in the United States created a new political philosophy that many called the Red Scare.

The Russian flag was red, and communists were referred to as reds, which is how the color red became the political identifier of the communist movement.

As a result of the so-called Red Scare, anyone who was labeled a communist was immediately suspect, no matter how honorable they might be or might be their cause. Conservatives tended to use this tactic to great advantage.

And since unions by definition were socialist in their organization, using collective bargaining as a primary tool, and paying everyone the same wage no matter what their skill level, they were vulnerable to being called communist, whether it was true or not.

But once the general public came to believe a union was communist, the workers lost the support of those who they needed the most: members of the establishment.

Jake, sitting near the door of the American Legion Hall, was startled out of his historical daydream as a booming voice called the meeting to order.

"Okay, let's get started," Osgood said in an authoritative tone. "We've got a lot of business to take care of."

The crowd quieted.

"For our first order of business," Osgood roared, "Association bookkeeper Brent Weaver will present this year's market report."

The audience responded with half-hearted applause, during which Weaver approached the podium to make his presentation.

The price of cotton was influenced by many factors, Weaver said, such as expected total production, world market prices, government subsidies, and local banking rates for crop guarantees.

World War I had been good to California farmers, when most European Allied production went into war materials. When WWI ended, farming prices dropped, partly because European farmers had returned to their farms. The Depression made matters worse for the farming industry, with bank failures and foreclosures increasing all the time.

The Farmers Association established harvest wages, which were based on all of these factors and the level of desired profit. Not a single year went by without an Association statement prior to setting the annual wage that told of the negative conditions which were driving the profit margin down.

Even in the best of years, farmers had explanations why the wages were so low. This year, the Depression was the major culprit, Weaver said, which is why the Association had decided on a 60-cent per hundred pound wage scale for the upcoming cotton harvest.

After some discussion among the members, a vote was taken and the wage was established. In about 20 minutes, the incomes of tens of thousands of workers up and down the valley were decided by the employers without consulting those who would be doing the work. Jake had witnessed this process for several years.

Following a brief interlude, during which the votes were counted, which was just a formality, the announcement was issued that the proposal had overwhelmingly passed. This year's cotton crop wage would be set at 60 cents per every hundred pounds of picked cotton.

At that point, someone in the audience stood and was recognized by the Association President.

"What about this strike talk?" he asked. "What are we going to do about that?"

The audience erupted into a roar. Farmers all over the Hall started to yell their contempt for the strike talk that had begun to emerge in the community after the previous day's union rally.

Osgood struggled to gavel the audience into silence.

Wham, wham, wham, wham. The audience would not calm down.

Finally, after a couple more tries, the pounding began to take effect.

The audience quieted.

"Let's calm down," Osgood said. "We can't accomplish anything if we can't control ourselves."

"What about this strike talk?" another farmer stood and asked. "Is there a chance it could happen?"

"I wouldn't worry about it," Osgood responded. "We've never had a strike in this part of the county, and we are not going to have one now. And even if one were to occur, it can't go very far. You can take my word for that."

The man sat down, apparently satisfied with the answer. The crowd renewed its discussion on the matter, but this time the discussion was more orderly.

Osgood let the discussion go on for several minutes before gaveling the meeting back to order.

"Believe me," Osgood added, "there is no way that some rag-tag union is going to railroad us on our own turf. It simply isn't going to happen."

Jake believed Osgood, of course, when he said that no union would succeed in this county, but Jake found it interesting that Osgood did not discount the possibility of a strike.

Jake knew Osgood well enough to know that he was a man who chose his words carefully, and by reading in between the lines, Jake became convinced that Osgood anticipated a strike attempt.

Osgood was also right when he said there had never been a strike in this county. And Jake knew that a strike could mean lots of trouble. The community would be scared to death at the thought that a Wheatland Riot could occur here, and Osgood would be able to use that fear to brutally break any strike attempt.

The problem was that innocent bystanders were usually the ones who paid the biggest price.

As the audience noise subsided, Jake heard a commotion just outside the building, and it became loud enough to attract the attention of several farmers sitting near the double doors at the front entrance.

Some yelling had escalated into pushing and shoving, and Jake moved toward the door to see what was happening, as did about 20 to 30 who were seated at the back of the Hall.

As Jake stepped outside, he could see Gordy standing between John Jr. and the smallish man who had addressed the rally the day before. Pat Chambers, the CAWIU leader, surrounded by several union members, including Veronica, demanded entrance into the Association meeting in order to present a set of demands.

John Jr. predictably became aggressive and was confronted by a couple of union members, when Gordy stepped in to calm things down. J.C. Osgood appeared -- surrounded by several of his supporters -- and took charge of the situation in his usual fashion.

"What is the meaning of this, deputy? Can't we have a peaceful meeting in this town anymore?"

He measured his words, of course, in order to put the union people immediately on the defensive. By making it seem as if the union was disrupting an ordinary meeting of respectable townspeople, Osgood could play the victim, making the union seem like the bully.

This was an important tactic, since there were several people standing around on the street who would spread the news of the confrontation.

"We are here on behalf of the workers," Chambers announced loud enough for the gathering crowd to hear him, "and we want to address the Farmers Association."

"This is a private meeting," Osgood said. "I suggest you leave immediately."

"You have not responded to our correspondence, and we feel that since the harvest is scheduled to begin tomorrow, this is our last chance to negotiate this year's wage scale," Chambers said.

"Correspondence? So, Osgood has known for some time that this was coming," Jake thought to himself. "What could be on his mind?"

"There is nothing to negotiate. The wages have been set," Osgood said as he turned and walked back into the Hall.

"It doesn't end here," Chambers said.

"It ends for now," Gordy interrupted. "You had better move along."

"I thought this was a public building," Chambers said. "You can't deny me access just because he says so."

"I think it is best if you just move along for now," Gordy repeated. "Nothing is going to be resolved by starting trouble."

Chambers reluctantly moved away and his group reformed across the street. He knew that a confrontation at this early period would undermine any possibility of successful wage negotiation. Public relations were an important aspect to this situation. Pat Chambers was as aware of this fact as was Osgood, although the farmers had other avenues to success as Jake would see.

Osgood had the upper hand for now, and Chambers knew it. He had to give in, because if the Farmers Association could successfully portray the union as the aggressor, the game would be over before it started.

But Chambers had made points as well. The fact that the farmers apparently didn't even want to hear what the workers had to say made it seem like the workers had a right to complain. The cat and mouse game was on.

What struck Jake as most interesting was that the "correspondence" Chambers referred to indicated that the cat and mouse game had been going on behind the scenes before now. Obviously Osgood was feigning ignorance to the press, but in fact knew everything that was happening. Jake shouldn't have been surprised.

Jake followed Chambers and his group across the street.

"Mr. Chambers," Jake addressed the union leader. "May I have a few minutes of your time?"

Chambers stopped and turned around.

"What can I do for you young man?"

For the first time Jake stood face to face with the CAWIU leader. Jake had heard bits and pieces about this man, but when he considered the fact that the sources of these bits and pieces were likely to have an inbred dislike for unions, he listened to the comments with a grain of salt.

Chambers was a monster. He was trying to wreck everything the community stood for. He was anti-American. Was all of this true, or was it that people who had something to gain by portraying Chambers in such a way were trying to create hysteria in the community?

Jake was several inches taller than Chambers, and it was hard to believe that this smallish man who looked like he could be anyone's frail grandfather could be the target of so much animosity.

"This is the local newspaper publisher," Veronica said. "Jake Rogers, Pat Chambers."

"I see. What can I do for you?" Chambers asked.

Chambers extended his hand. Jake noticed that the small man had a firm but not aggressive grip. He was nothing like the loud and boisterous J.C. Osgood.

"I would like to know more about your demands," Jake said, "and whether or not you plan to strike. The harvest begins tomorrow."

"As to your last question, it will be answered tomorrow. About our demands, we are simply asking for a better standard of living. We want to share in the prosperity of the local farming industry. Migrant workers are tired of living in squalor, and of being reduced to second class citizenry in their own communities. We want justice!"

"That sounds like a political argument," Jake said. "How do you intend to achieve those ends?"

"Our position centers on economics," Chambers said. "We want more money, better working conditions, and some respect. I would like to spend more time with you, but there is a lot to do before the harvest starts. Give him a copy of our demands, Veronica. Read that. We will have another chance to talk soon, I don't want to seem rude, but I have to go for now. Nice meeting you."

Chambers turned and walked away, followed by his entourage. Veronica stayed behind to go over the list she had given Jake.

"Do you mind if we walk while talk?" Veronica asked. "I am due for a meeting in about 20 minutes."

"I don't mind at all."

Jake looked at the list Veronica had given him and questioned its contents.

"This is a long set of demands," he began. "Do you see this as realistic? This wage demand, for instance. Isn't a dollar per hundred rather extreme?

"If I remember correctly," Jake continued, "last year's wage was about 50 cents per hundred. Isn't 60 cents a substantial raise?"

"The year before that, the wage was 70 cents per hundred," Veronica responded. "Last year it went down 20 cents because the farmers could get away with it. The sixty cents they now offer will barely keep us alive. It doesn't even account for inflation over the last few years.

"We want a future," she said, "like the farmers have."

They walked on for a minute or so. Jake divided his time between listening to her discussion and watching the movement of her lips.

As he watched her more, he had an overwhelming desire to touch her hair, stoke her neck, but he refrained.

"Our workers can, at best, pick two

hundred pounds of cotton in 12 to 14 hours." Veronica began again. "At last year's wage of fifty cents a hundred, that totals an average of a dollar a day, and the day is from sunup to sundown. On that income we are barely able to feed our families. Many of our workers are homeless or share roofs with others out of desperation. How much do you make? Could you live on a dollar a day if you only had four to five months work a year?"

"It would be pretty difficult," Jake answered. "But you know as well as I do that the farmers will say that paying a dollar a hundred will break them. What makes you think farmers are doing any better than you are?"

"Well, for one thing, they don't have to sleep in their cars or in tents, or along the side of the roads. They don't have to prepare their meals in the fields. They can afford to go to the doctor when they are sick, and they are at least able to feed their children adequately, send them to school and buy them clothes.

"Our kids have to work in the fields to help support their families. Without the added income from the children, many of our families could not survive. And when some of our families do manage to get their kids into local schools, they are put in rooms separated from white kids and given books that teach us that we are inferior. Have you ever been in our side of town?" she asked.

"Of course I have," Jake said. "But you can't blame your lives on the farmers. They have their problems, too."

"We don't begrudge the farmers a living; it is the treatment we receive that disturbs us. They make their living off the backs of migrant workers, and then toss us away like old shoes. They exploit us because they know we can't complain. And our women suffer from much disrespect. It is common knowledge among field workers that some women will have to sleep with their boss in order to keep their jobs."

"Has anyone ever asked you to sleep with them in order to keep your job?" Jake asked.

"Yes, more than once. But I didn't do it and I ended up without a job every time I said no."

"Some of my people are in this country illegally and have no rights," Veronica continued. "Illegals can get in trouble just for being here, but farmers who employ illegal immigrants make money with no worry about getting into trouble. Even those of us who are here legally can't get a fair deal in the courts when we have reasonable complaints against our employers.

"I know of many workers who were shorted on their pay-checks, and in many cases were not paid at all, but we couldn't complain to anyone.

"And when things get bad, farmers have the government to help them. Who do we turn to?"

"Why do you keep coming back?" Jake asked.

"Because farmers send recruiters to Mexico with offers of jobs and empty promises of better pay. They know it is illegal, but nobody does anything to them for breaking American laws. We cannot fight the American Government for turning its back on us, and we can't hold the government of Mexico responsible for not being able to protect us in this country, but we can fight the farmers for fair employment practices.

"Our best tool is to raise the awareness of the people who live in this town. We know there are a lot of good people here, both brown and white. But it is easier to ignore problems if they don't affect you personally.

Our job it to make people care."

They continued to walk. By now they were deep into the Mexican side of town, and Jake listened to Veronica as she described the problems of field workers. She pointed to the poor conditions in the Mexican neighborhood, and Jake looked intently at the problems she pointed out.

He had been in the poor side of town many times, but he had to confess that he never really looked at it the way in which he was looking now. The yards were well kept, even pampered, but few of the buildings were painted, many of the roofs were in need of repair. Few had piped-in running water, he knew, and some even had no electricity.

Members of the City Council said that funds were not available for trash collection in this neighborhood, but funds always seemed to be available for public services in other areas. Jake knew that much of what Veronica had been saying was true. This town, like virtually all others in the valley, was made up of two separate communities, one white and one brown.

Jake knew that non-white people had always had a very difficult time integrating into white communities. So much so that in one case "Negroes," as they were called, created their own township as a way of escaping the racism so prevalent in the San Joaquin Valley.

Jake had read about the community of Allensworth, an historical town just a few miles away, a so-called Negro community that had sprouted up and died out during the previous century. It was worn down now, but it stood as a testament to the race relations that had existed in this region ever since Mexico relinquished ownership after the signing of the Treaty of Guadalupe Hidalgo in 1848.

"Most of the people in Citrus Grove owe their living to the farming industry," she said, "but why is it that only Mexicans live like this? Is it because we don't care about ourselves like white farmers would have everyone believe?

"Do you think only white people want the best for their children? Do we suffer economically because we are lazy, like farmers say? We work 14 hours a day, hunched over in 100-degree weather, without proper toilet facilities or adequate food and water? You don't see many white people out in the fields. Have you ever asked yourself why?

"I know that because of the hard times right now more and more white people are turning to field work. But after the Depression is over, white people will return to their prosperity. We will not be included in that prosperity unless we fight for it.

"For us, every year is hard. We do not suffer just because there is a depression. Our lives remain the same no matter what the rest of the people are doing.

"And during the off season, we can't get work at all. Why do you suppose we move around so much? Do you think it is because we don't want to live like everybody else?"

Jake began to feel uneasy with the conversation. Her passion was apparent, and she was broaching subjects that made everyone in Citrus Grove nervous, but he was interested in what she had to say.

He had to admit that he never really investigated the point of view of the workers. The people who supported his newspaper weren't interested in what Mexicans had to say. Besides, spending most of his time in the uptown area tended to insulate him from the problems that existed in the Mexican community.

Veronica walked up to the front gate of a local residence and stopped.

"Here we are," she said. "I will be

leaving you now, but I hope we can talk again."

"May I come in?" he asked.

"This meeting is not for everyone," she said. "We don't want what we will be discussing here to show up in the newspaper. Please respect this."

"I understand," he said. "Will I see you again? I mean," He stammered, "will you be having any public union meetings soon?"

"Yes, we will. I will let you know."

Jake stood at the gate while she walked up the steps and into the front door, then he walked away and headed toward his office.

He wanted to get some of this down on paper while it was fresh in his mind. He thought about what Veronica said as he walked back. He knew what she said was true, but he had avoided facing reality. It was easier to simply look the other way and look out for himself.

But, did he have any reason to be proud of who he was and what he was doing with his life? Had his personal accommodation to the system resulted in a compromise in his self-respect? Who was Jake Rodgers? He was surprised that for the first time in his life he wasn't sure about these things.

Chapter Four

The following day Jake took his customary morning meal at the diner, expecting to hear the latest gossip. Discussing the goings-on of town was a favorite past-time in Citrus Grove. There was little else to do with one's free time. As it turned out, today was no different. The rumor mill suggested there was going to be a union demonstration at the gates of the Osgood Ranch, although nobody seemed to have any details.

He mentioned to Barney that he would love to go and see what was going to happen, but his old pickup truck was being worked on at the local mechanics shop. And it would take days to get the replacement parts.

Barney offered to lend Jake his car. He drove to his office to pick up a camera and some film and headed west for the Osgood Ranch.

The drive was about 20 miles, and at 35 miles an hour, which was all Barney's old jalopy was able to do, Jake settled down for what he thought was going to be a pleasant ride along the rows of maturing cotton.

The sun was already baking the valley,

even though it was only mid-morning. Temperatures were known to reach the triple digits this time of year on a regular basis. And it could be up to 90 degrees by nine o'clock. Jake could see the mountains in the distance, which was a rare occasion. There was usually too much dust in the air from the plowing to see much of anything.

Jake had promised himself for years that he would some day move to the coast where it was nice and cool. The heat was not to his liking, and neither was the winter fog for which the Central Valley of California was known. But after-all, time was on his side.

"The coast wasn't going anywhere," Jake thought.

He drove at a leisurely pace, with a clear view for miles, noticing some activity along the roadside up ahead. As he approached, he saw two men in cowboy hats and jeans wrestling with several crying women.

Slowing as he passed, Jake noticed that the men were tossing arms full of clothing onto the road. Overcome with curiosity, Jake slowed still more and turned his borrowed Model-A around. His news nose told him this could be interesting.

As he pulled up on the opposite side of

the road from the group, he could hear some of the yelling more clearly.

"I don't give a shit if your husband isn't here. If he thinks he can strike me and get away with it, he had better think again. No work, no housing! You people had better wise up before you lose everything."

"Please, mister, we have no place to go. You can't just throw our things in the street."

"You should have thought of that before you decided to make trouble. We don't tolerate commies around here. Get your things and get out."

Jake got out of his car and walked across the road. As he approached the man who had been doing all the yelling, he recognized Joe Muldur, foreman for Bixley Brothers Farms.

Muldur saw a man coming from his side and turned in an aggressive manner. He stopped when he saw who it was.

"Oh, Jake. It's you. I guess I am a little jumpy. It's these damn Mexicans. They are making me crazy. They can't understand why we won't let them live in company housing after their men walked off the job. We are evicting them because of the strike."

"So they actually did it. I'll be damned,"

Jake said.

"What do you know about it," Joe asked.

"Nothing. I just had a suspicion this would happen after interviewing a couple of union people yesterday, but it still comes as something of a surprise.

"I understand how you feel," Jake continued. "But it seems like this could be handled better. They still have their dignity. Have you tried to talk to the strikers? Maybe they would be willing to come to terms."

"Terms! They have been given the only terms they're gonna get. They can get their asses in the fields or sleep in the road as far as I'm concerned."

"From the looks of your housing, the road would not be a big step down," Jake commented. "Would you live in that shack?"

"Hell no," Joe responded. "But that is all they deserve. You sound like one of them. Maybe you should join the union too."

Jake could see there was no reasoning with Joe and his friends, so he withdrew to his borrowed vehicle across the road, cranked it over, climbed in and drove away.

He continued toward the Osgood Ranch for 15 minutes or more until he came upon what appeared to be another confrontation. In this case the police were on hand. What could be happening now? Had all the world gone mad?

He stopped about 50 yards before he reached the scene. He wanted to maintain his distance this time until he could completely assess the situation.

His previous experience brought out his journalist detachment. This time he was simply going to observe. There was obviously no percentage in getting involved, especially when the authorities were on hand. Let them deal with it.

As he sat in his car, Jake inched the vehicle closer so he could hear what was going on. His plan was to get as near as possible without attracting any more attention than necessary.

About two dozen vehicles lined both sides of the road. One more car could easily go unnoticed. Besides, he saw that the uniformed man on the scene was too engrossed in the situation to give another car that much thought.

Jake got within earshot of the yelling before getting out of the car. From what he could see, a man was standing on the back of a flatbed truck, yelling from the roadside at several workers who were at labor in the fields. At the same time, the deputy sheriff was trying to get the man to stop yelling. As Jake watched, the yelling got heated.

"What's going on?" Jake asked what appeared to be a bystander.

"Who are you?" the man replied.

"I am the publisher of the Citrus Grove Lantern, and I am here for a story."

"Oh, I see. Well, the man on the truck is trying to entice the workers out of the fields. He wants them to join the strike.

"The deputy has been threatening to arrest the man if he doesn't shut up. He's not breaking any laws. He is on a public road, and the First Amendment is still the law of the land as far as I know. So, from what I see, what he is doing is perfectly legal. Maybe it's against the law to speak Spanish on a public road in this county."

Jake sensed something odd about the man. He seemed out of place. In his early experience as a reporter, Jake had worked hard on learning how to be observant.

Jake noticed that the man was fairly well dressed, white shirt, dark coat and tie, although he had removed his coat and had rolled up his sleeves. His coat was draped over his arm and his tie was loosened, undoubtedly because of the heat.

He was a little pale and a little too soft to be a farmer. He did not have the rugged and tanned look that most of the farmers around here possessed. Rather, his dark rimmed eye glasses and thinning grey hair gave him a scholarly appearance.

What Jake didn't know at the time, however, was that this man's appearance was deceiving. Jake would discover before all of this was over that in the chest of this man beat the heart of a lion. Jake would learn that the energy and commitment of this man was unequaled by anyone Jake had ever met.

He also had some controversial opinions for a casual bystander in farming country, if indeed that is what he was. But if so, what was he doing out in the middle of nowhere? Few people were as outspoken as he appeared to be. Jake couldn't contain his curiosity.

"Who are you," Jake asked the man.

"My name is Solomon Wirinski. Why?"

"You seem to be involved in some way, and yet you speak very well for either a farmer or a field worker. May I ask what you are doing here and what interest you have in all of this?"

"Sure, ask away. I am a lawyer from the American Civil Liberties Union. We got word of this strike several days ago, and we anticipated this kind of activity would occur. I have been involved in several of these strikes. We are here to see that the rights of the strikers are preserved. Does that answer your questions?"

"Wow! Do you have any idea what you are in for around here?" Jake asked.

"Of course. This is not new to me. This struggle has been going on for years. I am an old hand at this. I cut my teeth on the Wheatland strike up north. A couple of deputies and a district attorney were killed in that one, and this has the potential for getting hotter than anything ever seen in this state.

"If you are out to make a name for yourself as a newspaperman, you might have had the story of the decade just fall in your lap."

"A name is not what I am after, but I would like to tag along with you for awhile, if that's okay."

"Fine. Do you have transportation?"

"Yes," Jake replied. "It isn't much, but it will get us where we want to go."

"Then it is better than what I have. I had to bum a ride to get this far. I was on my way to the Osgood Ranch when I got hung up here."

"The Osgood Ranch! That's where I was headed. But what about the man on the truck?" Jake asked. "Aren't you curious about what will happen to him? I thought you were a lawyer looking out for his rights."

"I am, but I already know what will happen to him. He will be arrested, and I will probably end up representing him in court, along with perhaps dozens of his associates. The Farmers Association around here owns the local police, and neither the police nor the farmers can afford a successful strike. The man will be arrested, believe me."

By now the events of the day were swirling around in Jake's head. He started out with the idea that it was a nice day for a drive. He had never really been confronted with a major story.

As a small-town journalist, he spent his time reporting on local high school athletics and ice-cream socials. The idea that a story of this significance would slap him in the face never entered his mind. In fact, one of the reasons he had avoided moving to the big city was because he was satisfied with being a medium sized fish in a small pond.

His position within the community was assured as long as he played by the rules. This potential story was more than he was prepared for. But for the first time he was getting a rush of journalism adrenal flow. This must be what it is like to be in the big time.

He was a little scared about the prospects, but he was also fascinated with them. As he drove his new found acquaintance to the Osgood Ranch, he began to feel that, perhaps, this was what he needed to emerge from the safe cocoon he had wrapped himself in.

As he continued to drive, Jake saw other men along the road yelling at workers in the fields to join the walkout. But there was something else totally unassociated from the workers that seemed to make the greatest impact on him. It was a group of Mexican boys who were playing in the dirt along side of the road, apparently oblivious to their surroundings, which sent Jake into a daydream about his childhood. He had been there. He had been one of those boys once.

The product of a mixed marriage in a time when being a "half-breed" was considered repugnant in the mainstream world, Jake had managed to sidestep the fact for years that his father had been Mexican.

His Anglo mother, Bertha, was an unusual turn-of-the-century woman who had been able to see past the skin color of a man she loved in a society that based its class structure largely on physical appearance.

The marriage did not last, because Jake's father, Jesus Enriques, turned to drink under the social pressure of the mixed marriage. They were accepted in the Mexican community, but they could not get out. Jesus had convinced himself that it was important to make the transition to the white world for his wife and son. But it was impossible, and Jesus buckled under the pressure. Jake's mother could not bear to watch her husband slide into a drunken oblivion, so she left and took Jake with her.

Jake had dark, curly hair and dark eyes like his father, but his complexion was neither brown nor white. He could pass for either Mexican or Anglo if one looked only at his skin. He nevertheless did not avoid the racism prevalent during the times. He learned very young that many people drew a stark distinction between the races.

His mother had worked for a white

family for a while when he was a boy. They were very nice people and were sympathetic toward a young white mother of a half Mexican child. His and his mother's lives were very simple. They shared a room in the back furnished with bunk beds. Jake slept in the upper.

They also shared a small dresser. They had no closet. The room was a converted store room that had not been originally designed to house people. They had no bath. They "washed up" out back. Their lives were safe and clean, even though his mother earned virtually no money. Her employer compensated her for her work essentially by feeding them and giving them a place to live. Their clothes came by way of donations.

Still, it was a step up from their field working days. Jake and his mother earned a living as migrant workers for a couple years before stumbling onto the job of domestic. So he knew first hand what the field workers were going through.

Jake and his mother had lived with the white family for a couple of years, and he had gone to school in an all-white neighborhood during that period. His mother had registered him under his given name of Juan Enriquez, and since he was the only Mexican kid in the school, it simply wasn't practical for school officials to segregate him from the white kids. Although he learned later that it was common place to do so in school districts that had a sizeable Mexican student population and the financial resources to do so. Besides, he spoke English well, something he had learned from his mother. And he had a fairly light complexion.

He discovered that if you were a little different it affected your identity in the eyes of others. His schoolmates simply called him the "Indian kid." They apparently did not know the difference between Mexican and Indian. Jake was not offended at being called an Indian, so he never bothered to correct anyone.

His mother had educated him to the fact that most Mexicans had at least some Indian blood, so it was probably true that he had some as well, although she did not know for sure. Jesus had always boasted of a proud Spanish heritage. Even in Mexico white was best, and many Mexicans sought to associate themselves as closely as possible to the European side of the Mexican racial structure, a practice that was deeply integrated into Mexican society during 300 years of Spanish colonialism. So Jake wasn't sure of his true ethnic identity while he was growing up.

Nevertheless, he found himself isolated from the rest of the kids. At recess he usually headed for a huge oak tree at the edge of the playground, where he sat alone watching the birds or something of the like. Growing up a Mexican kid in a white world was an experience he had hoped to avoid as an adult.

Jake was not clear on the chronology, because it occurred when he was still young, but at some point his mother had managed to track down her brother, Morgan Rogers. He took her in for several months until she felt it was best for her to take her son and find their own way in life. Morgan and Bertha never saw each other again.

But before she left, Morgan convinced his sister to change her son's name to Jake, which was a nickname for John, English for Juan. He also convinced her to re-assume her maiden name. So he became Jake Rogers.

He never questioned his mother's decision to begin calling him Jake. He knew why she made the change. They never discussed it again. But Jake could see how his life improved when he began to pass for white. And as more and more time elapsed, the further he drifted away from the Mexican side of his identity.

The Osgood Ranch was minutes away when the ACLU lawyer interrupted Jake's train of thought.

"You seem to be preoccupied," Wirinski said. "Do you have any questions?"

Jake snapped back to reality.

"Oh," Jake said. "No, I, well, it's not important. What are you expecting to see when we get to the Osgood Ranch?" Jake asked as he returned to the present.

"You know," Wirinski said absent-mindedly, "this is a beautiful valley. The potential is tremendous. If these farmers could only get past their racism and begin cooperating with their workers instead of viewing them as disposable human beings, both would benefit.

"But, then I guess I would be out of a job. Besides, it'll never happen until this country rids itself of its capitalist hypocrisy. Is this a nation of freedom and justice for all, or is that justice reserved for the money grubbing elite.

"But what am I expecting to see, you ask? I expect that Osgood and his kind will do everything they can to break up this strike. It probably can't happen any other way in this day and time."

"You sound cynical," Jake responded.

"Things don't seem that bad to me."

"That sounds like you are living on the right side of the tracks. You might see things differently if you were a Mexican in an Anglo society."

Jake considered his companion's words. They hit much closer to Jake's heart than the speaker knew. But Jake had spent years earning himself a place on the right side of the tracks as Wirinski put it. In some respects, he was living in the world that both of his parents had wanted for him and tried very hard to get for him. They both knew his future was very limited if he lived it as a Mexican man. And trying to straddle the two worlds would mean he would belong to neither.

Maybe he had turned a blind eye. But after-all, was this his fight? He was doing all right. He knew he would never get rich, but he had a good roof over his head, food on the table and beer money in his pocket. He was fond of reminding himself of that fact. But why should he jeopardize what little he had? He couldn't change the world.

The pair could see the main entrance to the Osgood Ranch ahead of them. As they approached, they saw a row of armed men standing in front of the white wooden fence that stretched across the entrance road to the main house, which was about three hundred yards away off in the distance.

There was an arch that spread over the entrance to the ranch that said "Osgood Ranch" in large, bold lettering.

"The size of that sign is exceeded only by the size of the ego of the man who owns everything behind it," Jake thought to himself.

Osgood was nowhere to be seen, but John Jr. was right in front of the group of men. Across the road was another group of men pulling picket signs out of the trunks of cars and off the backs of flatbed trucks.

The rickety vehicles looked as if they were held together by prayers. The modesty of the vehicles was rivaled only by the modesty of the clothing of the men who were lingering around.

"You might as well climb back into those cars," John Jr. shouted. "We don't allow picketing around here. This is private property."

J-J held the rifle he had in his hands in a threatening way. He loosely pointed it in the direction of the picketers. More toward the ground than directly at the men, but the intention was clear. It was meant to intimidate.

"The police are on the way," J.J. continued. "The fun's over, boys."

One of the leaders of the group looked familiar to Jake. He struggled at first to remember. Then it came to him. The man was with Pat Chambers outside the American Legion Hall the day before. Jake remembered that Chambers had seemed to call the man Blackie.

"He must be a union organizer," Jake thought.

"We have a right to do anything we want," the man returned. "This is a public road. We know you own the police, but you don't own the road. We will do as we please."

John Jr. fumed at the man's obvious lack of respect. He was not used to being talked to in that manner.

"Do you know who I am?" John Jr. asked the man who Jake believed was called Blackie.

"I don't care who you are," he answered. "It wouldn't change a thing."

"My father is John Osgood, and you had better watch your mouth."

"All I see is a big mouth redneck with a gun," Blackie said.

Jake was amused. He always believed

that John Jr. would not be as tough when confronted with someone who obviously could take care of himself. And Blackie was big, about Jake's age, in apparent good shape and obviously self confident. Jake took close note of this situation and filed it away for future reference.

As the two exchanged insults, Jake noticed a line of what appeared to be police cars a quarter mile in the distance and heading toward the group.

"This is going to be good," he thought.

The words between Blackie and J-J became increasingly heated as the police caravan arrived, and about a dozen uniformed deputy sheriffs piled out of their vehicles as the accompanying dust swirled around them. They assembled in an orderly group, wielding night sticks.

"It looks like trouble," Jake said in a sober tone.

"Oh, you bet there will be trouble," Wirinski said excitedly.

J-J attempted to bolster his sagging confidence and that of his farmer companions with words of encouragement, and almost on cue as a group they suddenly pushed forward into the picketers, shoving bodies away with their rifles. All at once, the shouting and shoving set both sides off and they rushed each other en masse.

Picket signs and rifle butts flew around as several men on both sides hit the ground bleeding from head and face wounds. The police charged the combatants and wrestled the most aggressive of the workers to the ground, with the aid of John Jr. and his cohorts.

After several minutes, the confrontation was brought under control, resulting in three workers in handcuffs and seated in the back of squad cars. Wirinski stepped to the front of the group and chastised one of the deputies.

"What about them?" he asked the deputy while pointing at the farmers. "Those men clearly violated the rights of these workers to peacefully demonstrate. This road is public domain. When those men entered the road and began their assault they broke the law. The men you have in custody are entitled to defend themselves. Is it your policy to arrest law abiding citizens while law-breakers go free?"

Jake winced as Wirinski went into his tirade.

"Who might you be, and what business is it of yours?" the unidentified deputy asked.

"I am a lawyer from the American Civil Liberties Union, and I will file a complaint for police harassment if you pursue this course of action."

"Another goddamn commie!" the deputy joked with J-J. "The place is crawling with them.

"If you don't mind," he said to Wirinski, "I will go about my duties. If you have anything else to say, you can say it in front of the judge. He probably needs a good laugh."

Solomon Wirinski stood there in obvious frustration, not noticing the look on the face of John Jr., but Jake noticed.

"You might have been better off not identifying yourself in front of that Osgood kid," Jake said as the two men returned to the borrowed car. "I could tell by the look in his eyes that he is going to make trouble for you, and probably for me as well for being with you."

"Nothing is achieved in this life without sacrifice," Wirinski responded. "I have seen his type before. They usually bark louder than they bite when the chips are down. You forget, I am an officer of the court."

"I haven't forgotten," Jake said. "You had better hope that John Jr. remembers."

The men climbed into the broken-down jalopy and headed back to town. Jake had a lot on his mind and said very little on the return trip. A side of valley life he had largely ignored had just landed on him like a felled tree. He had a lot to consider.

Chapter Five

Jake Rogers did not sleep well that night. He lay awake in bed, staring out the window and watching the stars with his hands clasped behind his head full of black, curly hair. His mind ran uncontrollably. There were many questions he needed to answer for himself.

Had he been hiding from the truth? Was it cowardly to ignore inequities in a system if there was nothing he could do? Was not self-preservation what this life was all about?

What about his personal history? Was his mother wrong for changing his name as a child, and thereby changing his identity? Who was Jake Rogers really, and where did he stand? There were too many questions.

It was well before sunup, but he could not sleep, so he halfheartedly crawled out of bed, put on the coffee, dressed and headed for his shop below with a full coffee cup in hand. The door jam to his apartment was stuck again.

"Damn," he thought as he struggled to open the door, "I've got to get that fixed."

He entered his shop and turned on the lights. It was still very dark outside, probably a couple more hours until sunrise.

He sat at his desk and tried to get started on the day. Fortunately, he had written several articles the day before, so he was pretty much on top of the next newspaper edition. But he had so much more to say.

The problem was that the words came hard this morning, which was unusual. Jake had never experienced writer's block, but then he wondered if he had ever truly been a journalist. Oh sure, he published a newspaper, but his articles had always been safe.

He was painfully aware of the realities of small-town journalism. The newspaper lived off the advertising dollars generated by the very same people who appeared in the pages of his periodical. And he learned early not to bite the hand that fed him.

He was also aware, however, that truth was the frequent casualty in such a system. But it had never bothered him before.

Jake sat in disgust as he stared at his typewriter. He could not continue. The diner was probably bustling. Farmers were usually up early, and the harvest was on full blast, so Barney was probably very busy, as early as it was. He decided to go have some breakfast and listen to the daily talk of current events.

Before he left, he wrote a note to Sally

saying he would be back as soon as he could. Tuesdays were busy days for the both of them, and she would be expecting him to be hard at it when she arrived in about an hour or so.

Occasionally when he had been ill in the past she wrapped things up on her own. She could not be as thorough as if both of them were working, but she knew how to fill in if need be.

They also kept a lot of space fillers around in case of emergencies, political cartoons, feature articles that had been submitted by local residents who liked to write for a hobby, and other miscellaneous items.

The real difference if Sally was in charge is that the newspaper would be heavy on society stories and short of the kinds of harder news items which were his responsibility. But Sally was very competent, and if he were to die tomorrow, she could manage to get some kind of newspaper out on her own.

Jake meandered toward the diner with his hands in his pockets, shoulders slumped and staring at the ground when a car pulled up along side. He looked up, and suddenly his morning seemed to brighten.

"You look like you lost your best friend," Veronica said. "Give you a lift?"

"Might as well," Jake returned. "Things have got to get better."

"What is the problem?"

"Oh, I just have a lot on my mind."

"Well," she said uncomfortably, "I can make your life a little easier. Hop in. I'll take you wherever you are going."

"I was headed to the diner," he said, "but I seldom eat this early in the morning. Where are you headed?"

"I am taking food to the refugee camp outside of Corcoran. You can tag along if you like."

"What camp? This is the first I have heard about it."

"And you call yourself a newspaperman," she poked fun. "Farmers in the area are evicting the families of workers who are on strike."

"Yes, I saw some people being evicted yesterday."

"Most of them are sleeping in groves or open fields," Veronica said, "but some are moving onto a field the union rented from a local farmer."

"What farmer in his right mind would rent space to union workers?" he asked with an amazed look on his face. "This is interesting. I think I will come with you, if you don't mind."

They drove along the countryside with the warm wind whistling through the windows, and Jake could smell a pleasant fragrance emanating from the exciting woman sitting next to him.

All at once, his problems were not so bad. No matter what was wrong, it would work itself out. There was no reason to let it drag him down, he thought to himself. Besides, it was going to be a nice day, as Veronica had suggested, and things could be much worse. All in all, life was good. The cup was more than half full.

"You mentioned that the property being used for this camp was rented from a local farmer," Jake said. "How did you come to find this man?"

"Are you asking me as a friend or a newspaperman?" she asked.

"Does it matter?"

"Of course it does. You know it does. We wouldn't want his name splattered all over the newspaper."

"I have no ax to grind here," he said. "We can keep it off the record if you like. I am just curious."

"You might get the chance to meet him

at the camp. If so, you can ask him anything you want."

The sun was beginning to rise, and Jake could see that the sky was as blue as he had ever seen it. And the cotton plants were blooming with white puffs of fiber. Miles and miles of cotton fields lay on both sides of the road. Anybody could see there were millions of dollars lying out there waiting to be harvested.

"What was the problem?" Jake thought. "Was there not enough for everybody?"

Jake could not help but be overly conscience of the magnificent woman sitting beside him. He had never been a big man among the ladies, even though he had had his share, he supposed.

But this woman was different. She was articulate, which was unusual among farm workers. She had a better than average vocabulary. This is something that Jake had noticed right away. As a newspaperman, Jake made a living through the use of language.

Yet he had not been able to precisely identify what attracted him to her. What was it about her that made him stir inside like this? Sure, she had a nice figure. But there was more. It was not just her looks. She was attractive. But she carried herself with a kind of self-assurance and dignity, and that translated into sex appeal as far as he was concerned.

He glanced at her voluptuous figure whenever he was sure she would not notice. She had called him on it before, and he did not want to embarrass himself again... or alienate her.

She undoubtedly had many suitors, and he did not want to push her. If she was interested, he figured she would find a way to let him know. It was not considered proper in Mexican culture for women to be too forward with men, but Jake knew that women knew how to get the lights turned on when they wanted to.

If she was not interested in him, at least he could bask in her closeness as long as it lasted.

After awhile, Jake saw emerging in the distance what might be the camp Veronica had mentioned. At first he strained to see what he could. As they came closer, the camp's configuration became clearer.

It appeared to be, perhaps, five acres, nearly square, bare of trees, with what seemed to be a water tank the size of a medium-sized truck at one end of the compound.

He began to make out what appeared

to be a tent-city, bordered by old cars, with laundry lines strung between makeshift poles protruding from the ground on angles.

They came closer and he could see poorly dressed children running around between the cars while the adults sat around on logs and benches talking and drinking coffee.

Jake and Veronica pulled up to the dirt entrance and were met by a couple of burly types who immediately approached the car. Seeing Veronica behind the wheel, they asked no questions, waved her passed and returned to their places on each side of the camp entrance.

Although entrance might be a poor word to describe it, since there were no walls or fences to keep people in or out. But the road came to a dead end at this parcel of property, and a makeshift entrance had been constructed.

She drove into the center of the compound, and they were approached again by men who appeared to have a purpose. This time Jake recognized some of them. One was Pat Chambers. Another man had been with Chambers at the American Legion Hall, and a third of several men who approached the car was Jake's old friend Nicholas Delgado.

"Senor Delgado," Jake said. "What a pleasure to see you."

Delgado approached Jake's side of the car and shook his hand as they exchanged pleasantries.

"Did you bring the goods?" Chambers asked.

"Yes, they are in the trunk," Veronica responded.

"Why did you bring him?"

"He's okay," she said. "He won't make trouble for us."

"Don't let your personal feelings get in the way of what we are trying to do," Chambers said. "We have too much at stake."

A couple of men went to the back of the car, opened the trunk, and began removing boxes marked "beans." Jake and Veronica got out of the car, and he saw that other boxes were marked sweet potatoes. The men also began to unload some fresh carrots and onions.

Chambers addressed Jake in a tone that suggested apprehension.

"Well, I guess you're here," he said. "We can't change that. Want to look around?"

"Sure," Jake said ignoring the obvious tone of dissatisfaction.

Jake, Veronica and Chambers began to

stroll around the camp, and Jake noticed that Veronica faded into the background. He knew that was due to her upbringing. As assertive as she might be on her own, she was still a Mexican woman. She stayed out of the way when the men talked business. As modern as she might seem at times, she still had some old school ways.

"How many people are here?" Jake asked.

"About three hundred right now, but we expect as many as several thousand before we are through."

Jake was visibly impressed. He raised his eyebrows and nodded his head.

"That many," he said. "You have been through this before."

"Many times."

"What about food, water and sanitary facilities?" Jake continued.

"We will do for ourselves. These people are used to little. A few inconveniences will not be noticed.

"You have to remember that even in the barracks facilities provided by farmers during harvest, for those who can get in them, our workers have no running water or electricity.

"Relieving themselves and taking showers are usually communal affairs. There is little privacy in field camps. We have not given up much by striking. Even the wages are only enough to get us to the next harvest, no more."

"Where will you go after the harvest is finished here?" Jake continued.

"Our next stop will probably be near Madera for a late grape crop or maybe apples," Chambers said. "By the first of the year you can find us in the Imperial Valley near Indio picking tomatoes and other vegetables.

"We might go to Yuma or as far south as Baja to pick winter watermelons, then move up the coast to Oxnard to pick strawberries. There is an early spring onion crop in Salinas, and by summer we are back here in the valley picking cantaloupes and summer watermelons.

"We can usually find work in grapes again in the late summer, and then, of course, the cotton crop kicks in around late September to early October."

"You seem to keep fairly busy," Jake noted. "But it means a lot of moving around."

The trio continued their stroll as Jake's eyes wandered. He saw dozens of people in desperate conditions, but he realized that if thousands were to cram into this plot of land, things would get much worse.

Even now, people were digging slit trenches in anticipation of the expected onslaught of people. Firewood was being trucked in and stockpiled. Large cauldrons were being set up under tarps to act as open air soup kitchens, and trash areas were being sectioned out.

The camp was being organized like it was a military operation.

"These people look as if they are preparing for war," Jake observed. "You'd think they were expecting an invasion."

"Veronica, this man is more perceptive than I realized. Maybe you should bring him back in a few days. I think he may be in for an education."

"I will," she answered, "if he wants to come."

"I think I will," Jake said.

The three continued their inspection of the camp in relative silence for the next fifteen minutes or so. Chambers could see that Jake was affected by what he was witnessing, and the union leader knew enough about human nature to understand when to make his pitch and when to step back and let pictures do the talking.

"What do you expect to gain by all this?" Jake asked.

"I have no illusions about winning major victories," Chambers said, "but at this stage of the game, winning a few small battles is progress. Winning the war will take, perhaps, generations. I have long-since resigned myself to the belief that total social, economic and political equality in the United States will not be realized in my lifetime."

"And yet you are willing to sacrifice everything without the hope of significant gain?" Jake queried.

"It is the fight that keeps me, and many of these people, going. Believing we are making a difference is our reward."

"Even if you are not making a difference?" Jake inquired.

"It's called social conscience," Chambers said. "Anyone who does not have beliefs worth struggling for is not alive, simply existing. The only thing a man leaves behind is his work. That is the only thing that is perpetual."

"You are leaving out us women," Veronica broke in.

Jake looked into her face with great affection, which Veronica immediately saw, causing them both to blush. Jake had not forgotten the remark that Chambers had made to Veronica in the car about personal feelings. Did she have feelings for him? He wondered.

Chambers caught the interaction between the two young people and begged his leave. He figured that Veronica could do more for the cause at this point. Chambers reconsidered his previous position. Maybe this needed to get personal.

"I have things to attend to," he said. "Veronica can show you around."

The couple found themselves alone as they slowly moved back toward the main entrance to the camp -- really alone, in the middle of hundreds of people -- and yet really together for the first time.

The camp inspection now seemed to take on the elements of a romantic stroll as the sun peeked over the Tehachapi Mountains. Jake fought off the urge to take Veronica by the hand.

He was the first to break the several minutes of silence.

"What did Mr. Chambers mean by letting your feelings interfere?" Jake asked, purposely placing Veronica in a corner. He was amused at her apparent loss of words.

Demonstrating her ability to recover, Veronica deftly dismissed Jake's question.

"I don't know what he meant," she said. "I think we had better head back to town."

Jake saw that he had been outmaneuvered, and he admired Veronica's obvious quickness. She was not like any woman he had ever met, and he decided to make an overture when he felt the time was right. A woman like Veronica did not come along everyday, and win or lose, Jake was sure he did not want to look back on his life and regret not knowing if there was a chance with her. Even if she rebuffed his advance, at least he would not allow himself to be afraid to take a chance.

As they came back to the camp entrance, people continued to pour into the compound, increasing the population by leaps and bounds. The influx of migrants from all over the county, however, attracted the attention of farmers; and where the farmers went these days, law enforcement was not far behind.

In only the passing of an hour or so, events had changed dramatically, and by the time Jake and Veronica reached the camp entrance, problems were already increasing.

The same two men at the front

entrance had now had been joined by other workers as several cars full of farmers arrived on the highway, and close behind were another several cars of deputy sheriffs. Jake noticed that some of the men were farmers who were displaying deputy badges.

Seeing his deputy friend, Jake stepped into the midst of the collection of adversaries.

"Gordy, what is happening? Why are you here?"

"Please don't get in the way, Jake. This is official business."

Jake looked at Veronica, who returned his glance with an understanding smirk on her face.

Several farmers moved toward the camp entrance when Chambers appeared with a couple of his union lieutenants.

"Can I help you gentleman?" Chambers asked.

"Yea," responded one farmer. "You can pack up this mess and get the hell out of the county."

The sound of subdued laughter emanated from behind the farmer who had apparently elected himself spokesman for the group.

"We have every right to be here,"

Chambers responded. "This is private property, and we have permission from the owner. What authority do you have to make this demand?"

"This authority," said the farmer as he threw a punch at the union man standing next to Chambers. The union leader backed well out of the way, not wanting to get into the middle of the fray.

As if by signal, the farmers pushed their way into the crowd of workers gathering at the camp entrance, and a spontaneous battle ensued. The fight was quickly contained, however, because the deputies stepped in immediately and began wrestling people to the ground.

In the course of only a few minutes, a half dozen camp residents were handcuffed and unceremoniously crammed into the back seats of squad cars.

As the groups separated and the sheriff deputies prepared to leave, Jake asked Gordy to explain what was going on.

"Why are you arresting these people?" he asked. "Everyone here could see the farmers started it."

"Jake, please take the advice of a friend and say out of this," Gordy said. "I have to follow orders, and I can't play favorites if I want to keep my job. If you get involved, I may have to take you in too. I will have no choice."

It did not seem fair, Jake thought. He could see no wrong in the worker's actions. He gave Veronica a puzzled look, and she returned his gaze.

"This does not surprise you?" she asked.

Jake watched the caravan of farmers and sheriff's cars as they disappeared into the distance in a cloud of dust.

Chapter Six

It had seemed like a long ride home after his visit to the camp, but when he returned to the office, his writer's block had disappeared. A strange thing had happened, however. His stories began to take on a different tone.

His inner feelings about his work also seemed different. This he noticed right away. The images of the people at the camp and their destitution danced in his mind as he wrote. Were these people asking for too much? This was the 20th Century. Shouldn't peonism be gone by now?

Jake did not have answers to some of his questions, but in this edition's editorial he would be asking questions that had not been verbalized in this town for a long time -- in fact, ever since his mother still lived. He knew there would be a price to pay. He had witnessed first hand what that price could be.

When his mother first came to Citrus Grove more than 20 years earlier, she became acquainted with William Henderson, the town's newspaper publisher. She was employed as a domestic worker, and he asked her to come to work for him.

When Bertha worked for the newspaper, she filled the same position that Sally now occupied. And since Bertha seemed to have a flair for writing, Henderson had given her a lot of responsibility right away.

She moved from doing light society stories to editorials in short order. And because of her personal experiences, she focused some of her attention on the problems between the races and the issues she witnessed in town. As a result, she was highly criticized.

This was also about the time that her health declined rapidly, and she died of tuberculosis within a couple of years, probably contracted during her period as a field worker. Jake was still very young and consequently never had to face any residual effects of his mother's public attitudes. But he stayed on with the newspaper. He had no place to go; he had lost contact with his uncle, Morgan.

Henderson fixed up an old store room at the back of the shop for Jake to sleep in. The older man had taken a liking to Jake. He was bright and energetic.

Besides, he had never married and was getting on in years.

He decided to train Jake to take over

the newspaper some day. And that is the way it worked out. Henderson died of cancer when Jake was in his mid twenties. It was almost like losing a father.

Jake never actually inherited anything. The building he did not own, and the equipment was not worth much. Nobody in the community disputed Jake's right to continue operating the newspaper. It simply never became an issue.

The next morning Jake decided to drive to the County Seat in Gunderson and visit the municipal court to view the day's docket. He wanted to see if any of those arrested would be in front of the judge anytime soon. Upon his arrival at the Hall of Justice he noticed on the posted agenda that virtually all of them would appear before Judge Stanley White during the morning session, which was going to begin within the hour. That meant he had time to look into other ideas he had working.

"This is going to be a very interesting day," he thought to himself as he descended the courthouse steps.

Jake headed over to Fred's Barbershop in the center of town. Fred had been around forever and prided himself in having the latest scoop on current events. Gunderson was the county seat with several thousand residents, but it was still small enough for everyone to know about each other's business. The women went to Cassie's Beauty Salon to hear about the town gossip. The men went to Fred's, although they didn't consider their talk gossip. To them, it was a simple matter of keeping abreast of political issues.

Jake had inherited the inside track to Fred's wealth of information from his adopted father. Anything one wanted to know about the inner workings of local politics could be gleaned from Fred with a simple ego boost. And the sweetest part of this situation was that Fred's was where most of the local deputies received their haircuts, since the shop was located right across from the Hall of Justice. The police station was right around the corner. It was a known fact that the oldest barber in town could make his scissors sing. Besides, deputies were interested in information too. The problem was that they tended to give Fred as much as they received.

Jake stepped into Fred's shop and saw him sitting in one of his chairs with legs crossed, his nose in a newspaper. Fred looked up and immediately recognized the virtual son of one of his best friends from the old days.

The old barber still had a sharp mind. Another reason people held such a high regard for the wealth of information he held. He was always reliable.

"Well, look what the cat drug in," the barber said with obvious affection. "Are you here for a haircut and shave - or just snooping?"

Jake knew that buying Fred's services would loosen his tongue faster than simply trying to pump him for information. Besides, he had an hour to kill, and renewing an old acquaintance was good journalism. Having a nice chat with an old family friend also would do Jake good. Things seemed too complicated these days. He climbed into the still warm chair just vacated by the venerable barber.

"Both," Jake answered, "and I guess I picked the right time."

"You have at that," Fred said. "It's been a terrible slow day."

Fred set to work with the efficiency of a man who knew his job backwards and forwards. He lost little motion when he was at his best. People came from miles around just for the experience. When things were busy, Fred zipped along like a man possessed. He even called out for the local shoeshine boy if he happened to be waltzing by the shop. "Fred's full service barbershop" was his motto, and he took pride in his work and standing in the community. Jake knew he would be missed when he passed on.

"I suppose you know about the full house over at the county jail," Fred began. "They've been coming in half a dozen a day ever since the strike started. The walls will be burstin' soon."

"Give me the story," Jake said, "and don't leaving anything out."

"The way I hear it," he said as he trimmed Jake's locks, "is that union organizers have been causin' trouble for the farmers and the deputies have been pullin' trouble-makers in right an' left. There's no way them commies will get away with stirin' up our mezkins. They have always been happy on their own side of town, and we don't need no outsiders comin' in and messin' things up, do we?"

Fred frequently finished his little speeches by asking for agreement as a way of validating his opinion. Anyone interested in what he had to say always agreed with him so he would keep talking. If you disagreed, he tended to clam up.

Over the course of the next fifteen

minutes Jake heard much of the story he had expected, very little of it being what he had not already heard many times over the years. One item that caught his attention, however, was the word that Solomon Wirinski was in town to represent the union men. That was enough to wet Jake's appetite. He knew from his first meeting with the outspoken Wirinski that sparks could fly in court today if things went as expected.

Jake begged his leave before Fred turned to the shave, apologizing for not coming around more often, and he rushed over to the Hall of Justice in time to catch Wirinski outside on the courthouse steps.

"Expecting a busy day?" Jake asked as he caught Wirinski by the arm.

"Oh, hello," the lawyer responded as he looked over his shoulder. "Are you here as a journalist or a farmer cheerleader?"

Jake was offended, but not as offended as he might have been a week ago. He was beginning to take a more objective look at himself and his role in the community, and he was starting to dislike what he was seeing.

Jake pressed on.

"I am here to see what's going to happen," Jake said. "I haven't decided where I stand."

"Good. Then come on in. You may get an education on the ways of farmer law."

"What do you mean by that?" Jake asked as he held the door open.

"I will see you inside. I have to take a final look at my arguments."

Jake followed the ACLU lawyer into the main gallery of the courthouse, and looked around as Wirinski disappeared into a room reserved for court officers.

Seeing the bulletin board where the day's agenda was posted, Jake strode over to it and began to read the list of names and charges. He recognized none of the names, but he did notice that practically all were charged with vagrancy, among other things. He saw nothing else unusual and entered the main courtroom, found a seat among the unusually large audience and sat down.

After a few minutes Jake detected a noticeable drop in the audience conversation and looked up to see several men being led into the courtroom in handcuffs, escorted by deputies. The handcuffed men were seated in what would have been the jury box if this had been a trial. Since this was only an arraignment, the box was otherwise empty.

Another several minutes went by when the bailiff entered and announced the arrival of Judge Albert Conley, and all present rose to his entrance. When he took his seat and sounded his gavel, the audience was again seated.

"Mr. Prosecutor," the judge bellowed, "call your first case."

George Green, local prosecutor for Tulare County, read off the list of several names, all of whom belonged to the farm worker union.

"Your honor," a voice was heard from the back of the room as most of the audience turned to see. "I would like to say a few words on behalf of the defendants."

"Do you have some interest in these men?" Judge Conley asked.

"I am from the American Civil Liberties Union, Los Angeles branch, and I just arrived in town. I plan to defend these men pending their consent."

The court room broke into quite a commotion, and the judge had to gavel the room quiet.

"This is a simple matter of vagrancy," the judge scolded Wirinski. "Why would you want to take up the court's time with such trifles?"

"With all due respect, your honor, justice is not a trifling matter. There is much more than vagrancy here, and with the court's permission I would like to demonstrate."

Red faced, the judge held in his obvious frustration.

"Is this your wish?" he asked the defendants, all nodding in the affirmative.

"Proceed," he said.

Jake knew Wirinski was off on the wrong foot by confronting the judge in open court, and yet he admired the lawyer's gumption. Everyone in the room knew this issue was not a simple matter of vagrancy, but it was probably not too smart for Wirinski to rub it in Conley's face, especially in public.

"Your honor," Wirinski said, "these men have not been arrested for vagrancy. They have been arrested because they are union organizers. Influential members of the farming community are behind this travesty. The defendants have been singled out by local law enforcement officials, and their arrests are being used as a strike-breaking tool. This is a flagrant violation of their civil rights."

"This is a serious charge," the judge said. "Can you offer proof?"

"Your honor, all of these men were

arrested while exercising their freedom of speech. Why is it that only union leaders were arrested and not a single rank and file union member? Also, why is it true that none of the defendants are property owners? It was the farm owners who were responsible for the confrontations that led to the arrest of the men present here today. Furthermore, the definition of a vagrant, as cited in the Tulare County Code of Justice, is a person with no visible means of support. I have looked up State of California employment statistics for Tulare County and discovered that nearly 35 percent of local residents are unemployed, and about 25 percent are virtually homeless. If this is so, the jails should be overflowing with Tulare County residents. This courtroom should be wall to wall with vagrants. And yet, all you see in front of you today as it turns out are union leaders. I challenge the prosecutor to offer an explanation."

"Mr. Prosecutor, would you like to respond to the allegations of our illustrious member of the ACLU?" the judge said sarcastically as he turned to Green.

"Yes, your honor. While true these men were engaging in union activities, they were arrested because they became belligerent in the face of law enforcement intervention."

"Are there any witnesses to this belligerence?" Wirinski asked. "Has a complaint been filed?"

"We don't need a complaint to arrest someone who is interfering with police officers in the pursuit of their duties," Green said.

Wirinski pressed his point.

"What were the police officers pursuing? What laws were being broken? The accused were on a public road trying to provide information to workers in the fields about their rights as workers. How does this warrant police intervention?"

"They were inciting a riot," Green snapped.

"Then why are they being charged with vagrancy," Wirinski countered, increasing the shrill in his voice. "By definition, virtually everyone on strike is a vagrant, with no place to live and no visible means of support. And yet only union leaders were arrested. I submit that this is a conspiracy between local law enforcement and a powerful farming trust that owns this county and everyone in it."

Jake wrote as fast as he could to get every word.

"You are, of course, exempting the

court from that charge," Conley said with a smirk on his face.

Wirinski paused, calming himself, and smiled in return.

"Of course, your honor."

"Mr. Prosecutor."

"Your honor," Green continued, "these men have been given a break with the vagrancy charge. We would feel justified in charging most of them with resisting arrest, interference with deputies in the pursuit of their duties, and trespassing. If my esteemed colleague would like a complete review of the cases at hand, I can probably add to the list of possible charges."

"Your honor," Wirinski responded, "there is no excuse for this. These men are being held on trumped-up charges in order to prevent them from..."

"Mr. Wirinski," the judge broke in, "the court has been patient, but you have failed to make a case for your accusations. Besides, this an arraignment, not a trial. I will place one thousand dollars bail on each defendant."

"A thousand dollars!" Wirinski exploded. "If these men had that kind of money, you wouldn't be able to charge them with vagrancy in the first place."

"If the defendants want to enter a guilty plea right now to save the court some time," Conley said with increasing volume, "they can pay a $100 fine each, and with a promise not to continue their provocative activities they will be released. However, if they persist in stirring up otherwise law abiding citizens into a strike, they will be re-arrested and charged with contempt of court."

"That is exactly what the farmers want," Wirinski shouted. "I think that makes my point. This is the most flagrant misuse of judicial power I have ever seen."

"One more word," Mr. Wirinski, "and *you* will be jailed for contempt of court. Bailiff, take these men and remand them into the custody of the county jail until bail is posted. I will set a trial time at a later date. Next case!"

Green opened the file on his next case as Wirinski exited the courtroom almost too quickly for Jake to catch him.

"Wait up," Jake said. "Give me a minute of your time, please."

Solomon Wirinski slowed his pace and let Jake close the distance, and they headed for the main double-door exit at the front of the building.

"Do you really believe what you said in

there?"

"That's a stupid question for a bright guy. Did my explanation of the circumstances make sense to you? You were there when some of those men were arrested. Were those men inciting a riot? If anyone was there to make trouble, it was the farmers. Why were none of them arrested, and who stands to gain the most if all the union organizers are in jail? Does it appear to you that the farmers own this county or don't they? Think about it."

"A conspiracy does seem to be a plausible explanation."

"You're catching on," Wirinski said in a disgusted tone. "I'd be willing to bet that Judge Conley and the prosecutor are married to sisters, or something like that. And Green probably plays golf with the Tulare County Sheriff. This is an old story. If you are really interested in objective reporting, I think it's time for you to wake up."

Jake realized this was not a good time to bother Wirinski. He was obviously agitated. Besides, Jake had a lot to do back at the office, and it was nearly noon. He had to get back to work.

Jake sat at his typewriter for hours as the keys sang their beautiful song. Writing was his first love, and he enjoyed it even during dull periods, but when he had a hot story, the rhythm of the keys were the music of angels; and he was on a roll.

Completely immersed in his work, he did not hear the tinkling little bell at the front door to his office as it announced the arrival of a visitor. And in this case, Veronica stood there for several minutes quietly watching him with growing affection as he pounded out his typewriter concerto. He was so consumed in his own thoughts, she did not have the heart to break his concentration.

Inadvertently, Jake looked up in thought for a brief moment and saw her standing there.

Startled at first, his eyes brighten immediately once he recognized who it was.

"Hello," he said awkwardly. "It's nice to see you. What brings you around?"

We are having a union meeting tomorrow night," she said. "I thought... that is," she stammered. "Pat thought you might like to attend."

He could see she was blushing, but she recovered quickly.

"I mean, I wanted to invite you," she corrected herself, setting her jaw in a somewhat over exaggerated show of self confidence.

"I would like to go," Jake said, "but I don't have a ride. Will you take me?"

"I will be by for you around six," she said as she turned for the door.

Jake watched her go, admiring her backside as she stepped out onto the sidewalk, after which he returned to his work with renewed enthusiasm. It was five o'clock now, and he still had much to do.

"Life is good," he said out loud to himself.

The next day flew by as Jake continued to hammer out his articles. Unaware that so much time had passed, he was still deep in thought when he heard the sound of a car horn outside. He happened to look at the wall clock and it read six o'clock.

Going to the window to investigate the sound, he saw Veronica sitting behind the wheel of a broken down Model A with a big smile on her face.

Jake waved like an excited teenager acknowledging his date to the prom. Stepping outside, he turned to lock the office door, and climbed in the jalopy with the dark-skinned woman. He made a conscience effort to collect himself.

The pair drove to the meeting place in the warm air and discussed the events of the day. Both of them were at first a little awkward in their attempt to make conversation.

"I was at the courthouse in Gunderson yesterday," he said uncomfortably. "That Wirinski character sure knows how to stir up trouble."

"He fights for what's right," she said. "That only results in trouble for those who would undermine justice."

"They arraigned your compadres," he said. "I'm afraid they did not fare well."

"Did you expect them to get a fair shake?" she asked.

"I admit that I was surprised at how blatantly the court ignored the facts of the situation."

"I am surprised that you were surprised. I would think that someone in your business would know more about what is going on in your community."

"When I first took over this newspaper," he said, "I wrote a story about a young, local man who had been getting into trouble in town and finally got a short jail term for his continuous unlawful activities. He was not a bad guy. He was mostly young and spoiled. His family has money and he seemed to think he could get away with anything. In fact, he usually did. This time, he slapped a cop and got 30 days. I applauded the sentence, and in the next week I lost several of my advertisers. His father, who was a local farmer of some influence, had put pressure on several local business people to stop their association with me. I suffered for several months before I could convince them to come back with me.

"Why didn't you tell the boy's father to drop dead?" she asked.

"Because that would probably have cost me my newspaper. I did okay for about a year when another incident occurred where a farmer was arrested for beating up his wife. In this case, I simply published the police log, but he nearly drove me out of business. I learned that to keep my doors open, I had to play ball."

"I don't think you want to hear what I think about that," she said.

"You don't understand, losing the newspaper would mean a total loss of local news coverage. How would going out of business just to be able to print minor stories have helped the community? At least some of the news gets into print."

"Yes, but it's censored news. Is that

what you want?"

"No, of course not. But what choice do I have?"

"You can do what's right, even if it has to cost you something."

"Being idealistic in a small town is foolish. Nothing will change. Where would it get me?"

"Maybe you should open a hardware store," she said.

For the next 10 minutes or so the two turned to lighter discussion. They talked about when they were kids growing up, and Jake felt a sense of connection with her that he had never felt before with any other woman.

Oh sure, he had girlfriends over the years, but he had not found one who thought about the same things that were important to him -- her discussion about the news business, for instance. She was right, and he knew it. But it had been easy to let his convictions slide when he felt alone in his beliefs. It is much easier to compromise when you don't know where you are going. And it was for that reason that he never truly felt a part of the community where he lived.

Of course, there was another, more obvious reason for not truly feeling like part of the community, his mixed ethnic heritage. But he had shut that reason in the closet a long time ago. And he had not been faced with it for some time, until now.

Veronica turned onto a dirt road and pulled up to an old barn in the middle of nowhere. Many trucks and a few cars were parked haphazardly, and she searched for an opening and parked.

Upon entering the building, Jake noted that benches had been lined up in rows, and a makeshift platform made from milk boxes and wood planks had been erected. Dozens of men, and a few women, sat among the benches talking in normal tones as Jake and Veronica moved to the front of the rows of seats. She sat down in front, as was apparently her habit, and joined in conversation with a couple people sitting next to her. They spoke in Spanish, so Jake allowed his attention to wander. He spoke some of the language, but he preferred for the moment to take everything in.

Farm workers continued to file in until the building was packed shoulder to shoulder. There must have been 200 people. A few children were present, and a couple of women carrying infants, but the vast majority of those in attendance were men.

Union representatives sat themselves on top of the raised platform, which was about a foot higher than the audience. Pat Chambers was seated with a half dozen others. Finally, one man, who had been called Blackie, rose to bring the meeting to attention.

"Bueno, compadres," he said. "Let us begin."

"We are here to finish plans for a major rally," he said. "As you know, we will be meeting in Citrus Grove in three days, this coming Saturday, to publicly denounce the unjust labor practices of the farmers in the area. You have been handed fliers detailing the specific information on where and when. It is important for you to understand that without a good turnout, out efforts will be lost. It is only through a show of solidarity that our objectives can be achieved. If we hope to have any success with the Farmers Association, they must believe we are all together in this. Are their any questions at this time?"

One man in the audience said that he knew the farmers were organizing a welcoming committee to disrupt the rally, and asked what the union was going to do about it.

"Nothing," Blackie said. "If we mind our own business, we will be all right. The farmers can't do anything if we remain peaceful. We have a constitutional right to meet publicly."

A general murmur of approval swept through the audience.

Blackie continued his discussion for the next several minutes on union demands for improved wages and working conditions, but Jake got the impression he was preaching to the choir. A public gathering in downtown Citrus Grove, where Saturday's meeting was to take place, would be much more of a challenge.

Suddenly, a burst of activity occurred in the back of the barn, and Jake heard a woman scream, accompanied with loud shouting.

Standing up and turning to see what was going on, Jake saw the double doors of the barn swing open to admit many men armed with clubs. Fist fights were breaking out and there was a rush of men toward the back. Jake climbed part way up a ladder to the loft in order to get a better view, while Veronica rushed to help a couple of downed old men to their feet and out of the way before they were trampled.

Benches flew, ax handles flailed away among the combatants, and Jake saw several men fall from the blows. He was probably 50 feet away, but from his vantage-point, he had a clear view.

What looked to be about three dozen farmers had broken into the barn, apparently to break up the meeting. Obviously underestimating the number of people inside, or the resolve of the people, the farmers were met with overwhelming force and were driven outside of the barn within seconds.

Jake ran to a side door to get a view from the other side of the battle, and he was met by a farmer who was running away with his arm dangling, apparently broken, and blood running down his face.

Pat Chambers and his lieutenants managed to get the crowd under control, and the farmers retreated carrying their wounded. It was a rout, and the farmers ran to their trucks to escape to the cheers and laughter of the workers.

Jake found Veronica nursing an elderly Mexican man who had been standing near the door. His heart was willing; he had undoubtedly been a lion in his youth. He had thrown a couple of punches, but his best days were gone, and he had just managed to get in the way.

"He'll be all right," she said.

"Let's go," Jake said. "I've got my story, and I have to get back to town."

During the ride back, Jake and Veronica talked excitedly about the incident. They laughed at the misfortune of the farmers who had obviously underestimated the situation.

It was still light out, but the heat of the day was diminishing, and the shadows of a setting sun were falling across the fields.

"It is hard to believe that such beauty can exist in the midst of such violence," he said after a brief silence.

Veronica did not respond, feeling that she could not add anything to his comment.

They pulled up in front of his shop.

"Are you going to work tonight?" she asked.

"Yes. I have to be done by about four in the morning in order to get the paper to the printer in time. So," he said as he looked into her face, "I guess I'd better go."

She leaned over and kissed him on the cheek.

"Don't work too hard," she said.

He got out the car and watched her drive away.

"What a day!" he thought.

Jake worked through the night to meet his deadline. He contracted his printing and distribution out to the Gunderson Globe, the largest newspaper in the county; and the Globe driver arrived early the next morning to pick up Jake's latest edition.

Rushing to the last minute, Jake was still pasting up his dummies when the driver arrived.

"No hurry," he said when Jake looked up from his work. "I am a little ahead of schedule."

Sam Wentworth was a driver for a local trucking company, but he moonlighted for the Globe occasionally. It did not pay much, but he really had nothing better to do. He browsed through Jake's stories while he waited.

"Wow!" Sam commented. "This is a hot one. Some people are going to go through the roof over this one about the court. Is it true that those union guys are getting railroaded?"

"Well, that's what happened," Jake returned. "I just reported the facts. I didn't make up those quotes. The lawyer is responsible for what he said, not me."

"This lawyer fellow has bought himself a pile o' trouble," Sam said. Some people don't want facts, Jake. You know that."

"Maybe that is the problem around here. Maybe it's time people faced the truth."

Sam looked over Jake's shoulder at the

story he was putting into place and read along.

"Jake, you aren't really going to print this, are you?"

"What?"

"This story about the riot at the barn."

"Yes, I am."

"This is really good stuff. I didn't know you had it in you. The farmers look like a bunch of idiots. But, you know what will happen when this hits the street, don't you?"

"Yes," Jake said, "but sometimes you have to do what's right, even if there is a price to pay."

Jake couldn't believe he said that, but he knew it was the truth. And, maybe it was time he faced it.

Jake wrapped up his news dummies and turned them over to Sam.

"See you next week," Sam said as he left the building with the box of flats under his arm.

Call Me Juan

Chapter Seven

The following morning Jake took his usual walk down Main Street to the diner, but today several people showed special interest in his passing. A couple of people whispered and stared, and a couple more commented about his articles.

The headline had read, *Farmers Get Bum's Rush!*

"A small but well organized group of men crashed a union meeting in Woodville Thursday evening armed with pick ax handles and were given a bum's rush by workers attending the meeting," the article said.

"Union representatives of the CAWIU led a meeting which attracted an estimated 100 to 200 farm workers, most of whom attended to hear the most recent information on the cotton strike that hit the valley this week like a bolt of lightening.

"Shortly after the meeting began, from two to three dozen armed men, some of whom are known to be members of the local Farmers Association, forced their way into the barn where the meeting took place.

"Surprised but undaunted, farm workers

met the threat and a general melee resulted, with several farmers being injured in the process. As chairs and benches flew across the barn, the farming faction was driven from the dwelling, nursing wounds varying from bruises and contusions to a reported broken arm.

"As they rushed to their vehicles for their escape they had to dodge a rain of bottles, cans and rocks to the laughter of the workers who had turned them back.

"Union members said the farmers had undoubtedly underestimated the conviction of the workers or they would have had greater respect for the superior numbers of meeting attendees.

"Asked if union activities would be curtailed in the wake of escalating farmer violence," the article concluded, "one union organizer who asked not be identified said, "'If this is the best they have, I can't see anything to be afraid of.'"

Bill Franklin, a black man who had been crowded off his land by a local farming trust, and now made ends meet as a part-time carpenter and handyman, was first to congratulate Jake about his recent edition.

"It's about time people faced what is going on around here," he said. "Maybe there will be some changes. You might make a newspaperman yet."

Jake did not like that last comment, but he could not blame Bill. He was a good man and a hard worker, but Jake had to admit that as a black man Bill did not have a chance in this town.

Admitting that fact to himself seemed to mark a turning point in Jake. For the first time in many years he looked back to his childhood and what he and his family went through.

Mixed marriages were disgraceful, so most people during his childhood thought, and many still did. In fact, Jake knew that several anti-miscegenation laws were still among the California legal codes dating back to the late 1800s. These laws prohibited marriage between various ethnic groups.

Jake and his family was continually victimized as far back as he could remember. In school his white friends criticized him if he acted too Mexican. Even his white mother and Mexican father encouraged him to act as white as possible for fear he would be ostracized.

"Be like them; that is the only way you will make it in this world," his dad had told him at every opportunity.

He was sure these problems

contributed to his dad's alcoholism. And when his mother died, Jake lost connection with the last person he felt he could turn to. But he had always remained optimistic about himself and future. For the first time in his life, Jake felt feelings of anger well up inside him. Not that he blamed anyone in particular, but that he had denied himself so much for so long.

Moving away from the town of his birth had changed his life. Because his skin was light, he was able to pass as an Anglo in Citrus Grove upon his arrival, and his mother had been white, so nobody questioned his race. Since then, he did not talk about his past, realizing that if people knew his father had been Mexican, they would react to him differently.

Despite the fact he had not made a special effort to hide his true identity – changing his name had not been his idea -- he had nevertheless not openly embraced his Mexican side either. Now, he felt a sense of shame, even though he knew he was living the life his parents wanted for him. By denying who he really was, even to himself, he was paying a bigger price than anyone knew.

Jake continued to circulate around town as was his usual custom on publication day. As might be expected, several members of the farming community also had things to say about his news coverage. In fact, Jake ran into Gus Richardson coming out of the bank. He had been one of the farmers who had been sent packing the day before at the union meeting.

"I read your account of yesterday's union riot," Gus said. "You sure made a mess of it."

"I just wrote what I saw," Jake said.

"Yeah, but you made us look bad. Those greasers should have been arrested for inciting a riot."

"They didn't incite anything. In fact, there would have been no trouble at all if the farmers hadn't started it. You had no legitimate business there to begin with."

"You had better watch your step," Gus said. "You are in danger of making some powerful enemies in town."

Jake watched Gus walk away. He knew the farmer was right. Maybe Jake delighted in writing the truth for a change. He somehow enjoyed sticking his journalistic thumb in the eye of the farming community. It had been a long time in coming. But he also knew there would be a big price-tag attached to his honesty.

The weekend passed, and Jake began his

early week news gathering activities of marriage announcements, obituaries and a list of events for the paper's social calendar.

The last edition was not forgotten, however. Jake continued to overhear comments about the union activities. Most, of course, were pro farmer. In some cases, interestingly enough, he was encouraged by a few people who quietly approached him and congratulated his coverage. He began to realize that others had similar feelings about the farming industry's political and economic stranglehold over local public opinion. Although they also knew the cost of being too public about their feelings.

The Farmers Association had replaced the railroads of the previous century as a coercive force over the average person. These emerging farming trusts were squeezing out the white family farmer as well as intimidating town residents into supporting farmers for local elective office. The Mexican farm workers were just a part of the list of casualties. There were decent, honest, hardworking white people who were victimized as well.

Anyone who would not go along with the will of the Farmers Association found themselves either out of business or out of town. Farmers could band together and boycott anyone into economic oblivion with the full support of those who depended on the farming industry for their livelihoods. And that was about everyone, from the local hardware store owner, to the local tractor sales owner, to the feed store owner. All of these people played by the Farmers Association rules or suffered the consequences, which usually meant financial destruction.

Even if they might have been sympathetic to the plight of the farm worker, they dared not to speak out in public. If you sold gas, tires, pesticide, or anything else that the farming industry purchased in relatively large quantities, you would be expected to play by the rules of the Farmers Association.

When Jake returned to his office, he saw John Jr. standing across the street in front of the Mercantile Store. J-J disappeared into the store as Jake unlocked the door to his shop. As Jake began to organize the information he had been gathering all morning, the little bell rang and John Osgood entered. Osgood sauntered up to the counter with a smile on his face, which was his usual way, with John Jr. coming in behind.

"Well," Jake said, "the Osgood family.

What brings you here?"

"You have been a bad fellow," Osgood said, "and I want to express my displeasure. It seems you have trouble knowing on which side your bread is buttered. You know that a word from me is all it will take to have you shut down?"

"I know," Jake said, "but I don't think that would be wise. There are not many people in town who would stand up for a bunch of farm workers, but there are a lot of people who would stand up for the First Amendment. This strike looks like it is going to get messy, and you will need the support of the community. Muzzling me will hurt your cause."

"Maybe I underestimated you, Jake. But there are lots of ways of dealing with your kind."

"Yeah, maybe I'll just meet you in an alley some day," John Jr. interjected.

"Do you let this loud mouth son of yours do your dirty work," Jake said to Osgood. "Maybe he is good at beating up 16 year old kids, but what would he do against a man."

John Jr. suddenly went at Jake and tried to climb over the counter when his father shouted him back into his place. Jake chuckled to himself at the display. J.J. was well trained, Jake thought, kind of like an old dog his father once had.

"J-J," his father said, "this is not the time or place for rough stuff. I'll give you one more chance, Jake. If you temper your language regarding this strike, I'll see to it that your business improves. Who knows, maybe in a few years you might be able to purchase your own building, if you catch my drift. Otherwise, don't expect to be in business when this is over."

"I'll take that under advisement," Jake said as Osgood and J-J turned for the door and left. "But meanwhile, let me advise you to keep your pet under control before he bites someone. He might get bitten back."

J.J. turned and tried to go after Jake one more time, but the father shouted him into submission again.

"It's alright J.J.," Osgood told his son. "Your chance will come."

The two of them walked out the door.

Jake pondered Osgood's words. He fully understood that if he continued this kind of treatment of the situation in a way that was unflattering to the farmers, he would have no future in this town. On the other hand, maybe there were enough good people in this community who believed in doing the right thing. It was a gamble, but he had played it safe for too long. Cost or not, it was time to print the real news.

During the next several days, area newspapers reported other incidents around a five county area. Union organizers were filling up the jails, typically charged with vagrancy.

Minor incidents of violence between farmers and farm workers ended with union members in jail on various charges. In one case 16 workers were arrested for "trespassing" by "special deputies" who were aiding the police.

Newspapers, from as far away as San Francisco and Los Angeles, began to publish reports on threats made by farmers to end the strike "by any means necessary." In some cases, representatives of the farming industry suggested the use of vigilante justice to "solve" the increasing problems that apparently were becoming too much for the local legal system.

The violence escalated until a news report from an out-of-town newspaper printed a story that Kern County was issuing gun permits "on demand." The story did not specify who were obtaining the permits, only that a record number had been issued. When reading the story Jake knew that farm workers were not getting gun permits.

Another Kern newspaper story suggested that farmers all over the valley were organizing groups of "special deputies" that would aid police in their job. After reading this story, Jake knew who the gun permits were going to.

The official police stance on this threat was to discourage the use of vigilante justice, but the reality, Jake was sure, was that the activities of farmer vigilante groups would be winked at by the local police and court systems. There was little doubt that the problems were getting of control, and Jake knew that the Farmers Association was behind much of the violence. This was exactly what Wirinski had warned.

Other stories stated that in a five-county area an estimated 20,000 or more strikers were involved in the walkout of the cotton harvest, an astonishing number when one considers that virtually none of the communities affected contained a population anywhere approaching that figure.

After about 10 days the strike seemed to settle down. Most of the union organizers were in jail, which slowed organizing activities considerably. Wirinski had called it. The best way to break the strike was to remove the union leadership.

"Without a head, the body dies," as Wirinski had said earlier during an interview.

One other story caught Jake's eye. It was about the Corcoran refugee camp. He had not been there since his first introduction by Veronica a couple of weeks earlier, and he had a standing invitation from Pat Chambers to return. Maybe this was the time. He managed to coax Barney to part with his old car for the day, and Jake hit the road to Corcoran.

He hoped to run into either Chambers or Veronica, since the camp was the only place where a large number of workers could be found. The camp had become a place where strikers could go to receive some help. A soup kitchen was feeding about four thousand people a day, said one newspaper story.

But from a union standpoint, the camp undoubtedly had also become a place where many strikers could be given information about the progress of the strike and plans for future picket projects. It was the largest single concentration of agriculture workers in California. Most of the other strikers were hard to reach because they were living in cars, groves and along road sides, scattered around hundreds of square miles of the San Joaquin Valley.

Jake was not prepared for what he found at the camp. As he pulled up to the entrance, he was met by union members acting as guards. One guard remembered Jake and had instructions from Pat Chambers to allow the newspaperman unlimited access. Jake parked at the edge of the camp and went inside the makeshift barriers made of wood piles and parked cars. It was beginning to look like a prisoner of war compound.

As Jake walked around the camp, what he saw made him feel terrible. He had personally experienced poverty, but the camp was a disaster. He saw a small group of men and decided to ask a few questions.

"Como estas," Jake said as he approached a man sitting on a log with a cup of coffee in his hand. "Hablas Ingles?"

Jake's Spanish wasn't very good. He hoped to find someone who spoke English.

"Si," was the reply from one of the other men. And Jake exhaled a sigh of relief.

"Bueno, what is your name?" Jake asked.

"Francisco," the man replied.

"How are you getting along?" Jake asked the man.

"Not so well."

"Do you have enough to eat?"

"We have very little," the man said. "People are getting sick. One boy of about three years went to the hospital yesterday. I think he died."

Jake wondered why he had not seen anything in the morning news about this.

"A woman was found by the road near town," the man continued. "I think she is dead also."

"Do you know where I can find Pat Chambers?" Jake asked.

"He is in Citrus Grove, I think, making plans for a rally."

Bidding the men good luck, Jake continued to move around the camp. It was about five acres in size, with different sections set aside for different services. In one area slit trenches had been dug to act as latrines. At another end of camp, a garbage heap was beginning to pile up. The flies around camp were out of control. Clean water was scarce, and the smell at certain times of the day Jake discovered was nearly unbearable. The planning of this camp was not very good, Jake concluded.

He had seen enough and headed back to

the borrowed car intending to drive to Citrus Grove and ask Pat Chambers what was going to be done about this mess.

As he approached his vehicle, an official looking car with Kings County written on the side pulled up with a police escort. Jake decided to postpone his trip to Citrus Grove in favor of witnessing the next few moments. He thought this could be important.

The Kings County Health Department official, Richard Montgomery, handed the guards at the camp a notice to vacate the property. Just about this time, Pat Chambers pulled up with several of his union people. Chambers had undoubtedly gotten word of the eviction and was there to represent union interests. Jake moved closer.

"Please let me have that," Chambers said to his worker. "You moved pretty fast."

"The Corcoran Chamber of Commerce issued a call for County authorities to deal with the conditions at this camp," Montgomery said. "And yesterday the Corcoran City Council issued a resolution to press authorities to have the camp vacated. Residents are concerned that cholera may be breeding here."

"That is farmer propaganda and you know it," Chambers said. "You know full well that the report of cholera turned out to be a case of measles, and it is irresponsible for a health official to continue to promote this outrageous rumor. I guess we can add your department to the farming conspiracy to break this strike."

"I resent that," Montgomery said. "Look at the conditions at this camp. How can you let these people live like this?"

"Are you saying that when you close this camp they will be better off living on the road? They have food here, and the farmer thugs roaming the roads with guns and belly clubs dare not come here. We are too many," Chambers said. "On these premises, these people are free to come and go as they please without fear. Are you going to protect them after you force them off this property?"

"Where they go is not my concern," Montgomery said. "I have a lawful order to vacate this place, and these deputies are here to arrest anyone who does not comply immediately."

"Ah, yes, what is a *lawful* order without the Gestapo to help you enforce it?" Chamber said.

Another car rumbled up in a cloud of smoke, and Solomon Wirinski hurried to the group.

"I am the legal representative of this group and the property owner here," Wirinski announced to Montgomery, "and I have a 48-hour stay of execution of your Notice to Vacate. We have clean water on the way, and trucks to cart out the garbage."

Jake noticed that a couple of the deputies were in civilian clothes. They were undoubtedly special farmer deputies Jake had been hearing and reading about. No doubt this situation would be immediately reported to the Farmers Association. Jake was continually astonished at how well organized the farmers were.

Montgomery looked at the injunction that Wirinski presented to him.

"This order also states that I have the authority to oversee improvements, and that if I am not satisfied with the progress, my authority is restored to have you evicted within 24 hours. I want to tour the camp and direct the clean-up plans."

"Fine," Chambers said. "We want to cooperate."

The situation apparently diffused, the deputies left, including the special deputies, while Chambers, Montgomery, and Wirinski walked around the camp. Chambers invited Jake to join them.

"Look," Montgomery said when out of earshot of anyone who could convey his words to the deputies, "I have nothing against you people," he said. "I simply have a job to do, and this camp is a potential source of disease. My future employment may depend on how I handle this situation. Please understand my position. I have a family to feed. And jobs these days are pretty hard to come by."

"I am glad you are not taking sides in this Mr. Montgomery," Chambers said, "and I apologize for what I said earlier. No hard feelings, I hope. We don't have many friends around here. But we have a lot of families here as well. And all they are asking for is what you already have: a decent job for a fair wage."

"No hard feelings," Montgomery said. "Let me help you with your plan. I am sure we can make this camp presentable enough to satisfy my department heads. If we can do that, the farmers' hands will be tied regarding the camp."

For the next half hour or so, Montgomery toured the camp and offered suggestions on how to make the camp health code compliant.

"Don't let the slit trenches get so full before they are covered up," he said. "Dig new trenches frequently. And remove the trash daily. That will cut way down on the fly situation. Cover your soup cauldrons. Build more shade canopies. And for God's sake, haul in all the fresh drinking water you can. Boil any water that has been sitting around for more than 24 hours. Some of this may be tough, especially hauling away the trash. But it has to be done."

"Thank you for your help," Chambers said. "We will do everything we can. Please work with us on this. Our finances are thin, and we have few vehicles and very little petrol."

"I understand," Montgomery said. "I will return to the camp this evening to see how you are doing. I will give you every consideration I can. But we can't have any more hospitalizations. We already have had two deaths associated with this camp. One was probably from tuberculosis, which was no doubt a pre-existing condition. But the press is right on top of this. We must do everything we can to improve this camp."

"We give you our word," Chambers said. "And thank you."

"Don't mention it," Montgomery said as he walked toward his car.

"Well," Jake asked, "do you think you can clean this place up? This is really a mess."

"Actually, we knew early yesterday that this was going to happen, and we have already made plans. This is not our first strike. We have been through this before."

"Then why did you wait?"

"Off the record?"

"Okay," Jake said.

"It is necessary to bring as much attention to our plight as possible," Chambers said. "The only chance we have is in the public opinion arena. We have no guns, and no special deputy police force. We have no legal and political support locally. All we can hope for is to bring this situation to the attention of state or federal officials who can exercise some influence over the locals. I prefer that you did not print that, since exposing our tactics is not part of our overall strategy. You can understand that."

"Of course," Jake said. "But people's lives are at stake. What if more people die?"

"People's lives have always been at stake, their futures, their children's futures. It is about time the general public sees that,"

Chambers said. "Now, if you will excuse me, we have a lot of work to do."

"Sure," Jake said as he shook hands with the mild mannered man.

Jake was lost in thought as he returned to his car. Of course lives, and not just livelihoods, were at stake here. He should have known that. Maybe that is what happens when you lose yourself in ice cream socials and wedding announcements. You lose touch with the bigger picture.

Jake hoped he was not making excuses for himself. He had made his choices, but maybe it was time to re-evaluate those choices. If he continued down the path he was currently going, he knew his future in Citrus Grove was limited. Osgood had made that clear enough.

Maybe Veronica was right. Maybe he would be happier as the owner of a hardware store. No, he was feeling sorry for himself. He was young. The story of his life had yet to be written. When he got old, was he going to be happy with the way he lived his life? Veronica had made him think about a lot. She had been a good influence. He had not been happy, only going through the motions.

He knew what had happened to the Delgado boy, and it was probably John Jr. who had beaten him up. He was the only one in town who was capable to that kind of thing, but there was no one who would say it out loud.

The boy had been injured too badly to name the assailant, so the official record said it was probably a transient -- very convenient. What were the chances that a total stranger could have done that? There would have been nothing to gain. The boy had carried no money. No, it had to be someone who had a grudge for some reason. John Jr. hated anyone with brown skin. Not that he was the only one, but he was among the few in town who was violent enough to do something like that.

But why was nobody willing to do anything about it? Probably for the same reason people stood by and allowed these so-called special deputies roam the countryside beating up union members and breaking into lawful and peaceful union meetings. Were there any good people left in this valley? Of course there were. That health official seemed a decent man. And, Jake was sure there were more.

But the Farmers Association was too powerful. They got public officials elected and un-elected. The country sheriff, the district attorney and the municipal judges were all elected officials, and without the money contributed to their campaigns by the local farming industry, none of them would be where they were now. No wonder Wirinski was so frustrated.

The only hope that justice would prevail in this strike was through a free press, and Jake seemed to be the only newspaperman in the five county area where the strike was occurring who might be willing to speak out.

Out of town newspapers may print the truth without fear of recrimination by local farmers, but the out of town papers did not count here.

It may cost him is livelihood. But Jake decided that how he felt about himself was more important than protecting his meager income. He was the one who had to look at himself in the mirror every morning. He was going to forge ahead and do what he thought was right… and leave his fate to the gods.

Call Me Juan

Chapter Eight

For the next few days Jake went about his business without incident. His newspaper coverage continued to report on confrontations between strikers and farm-owners. The Farmers Association increased its public outcry against union activities while the jails continued to fill to over flowing.

One event, however, would overshadow all of the others. The CAWIU had planned a massive public rally designed to promote unity among the strikers and at the same time give a message to the Farmers Association that the union was here to stay. Jake expected this event to be the largest of its kind ever seen in the great Central Valley of California. Hundreds, perhaps thousands, of workers from miles around were expected to participate.

The rally was to be held at the Union Hall near the park in downtown Citrus Grove. The building had always been called the Union Hall, although nobody knew why. There had never been any union activities in the building as far as anyone remembered.

Jake reasoned that the reason for its

name probably had something to do with the fact that the building had historically been used for a place where people could get together. These days it was mostly used by the Mexican community for dances, weddings, and other social activities. The building had long been abandoned by the white community, probably because it was old and in disrepair.

It was a bright and sunshiny Tuesday morning, typical valley weather. Jake came early as usual in order to watch events develop. He was by habit an early riser and typically was out of his apartment long before the town came to life.

He watched as banners were attached to the front of the Union Hall. The banners exhibited slogans like "Justice for all" and "A Fair Day's Pay for a Fair Day's Work." Jake knew that if these banners had been placed on the buildings the night before, they would not still be there this morning. He suspected that union leaders understood this as well, which is why they rushed around the last minute with these finishing touches.

Jake had a short but pleasant discussion with Veronica before she went into the building. She was busy with her activities, and Jake had a lot to do, so neither of them had much time for socializing.

Jake circulated among several of the businesses surrounding the Union Hall as he solicited comments from local merchants about the implications of the meeting and the strike in general. He knew these business owners very well, since part of his job called for him to report on local Chamber of Commerce functions.

Most of the comments he received indicated favorable public opinion toward the farmer's side of the dispute, although the business owners generally agreed their businesses received a boost from the seasonal purchases by migrant workers.

They also reluctantly agreed that if the workers received better wages, their sales would improve even more during the harvest; although the business owners Jake spoke to worded their comments carefully, since they knew of the potential fall out if they said anything that may be misconstrued as pro-worker.

A recent advertisement in a regional newspaper left little doubt of the intentions of the farmers to retaliate against anyone who was out of step with their points of view.

"It has come to our attention," the

advertisement read, "that some people in Tulare County communities are harboring criminals in our midst. All communists who are trying to undermine our way of life here in the San Joaquin Valley must be exposed and driven out. And anyone who supports these criminals will have to face the consequences for their sins. Signed, the Tulare County Farmers Association."

The ad filled an entire page with similar threats, including an eighth-page political cartoon reflecting caricatures of Vladimir Lenin and Joseph Stalin staged in roles portraying the union leadership. The implication was clear: anyone who even appeared to vary from the lock step of farmers gambled with their futures in this county.

The ad had been released after the Farmers Association learned that some community members were contributing food and old clothing to workers who were going door to door asking for help to support themselves.

During the Depression, single men commonly moved from house to house asking to trade a day's work for a meal or two. But when it was discovered that union members were collecting food and clothing for the workers at the Corcoran camp, the Farmers Association decided to intervene.

The result was that virtually all destitute victims of the Depression for miles around suddenly found themselves inadvertently embroiled in the dispute. As a result of the advertisement, giving to the poor came to a screeching halt, since people who might want to help the destitute had no way of knowing if the person coming to the door for a handout was a member of the increasing hobo population or a member of the CAWIU.

But being Mexican was a dead giveaway on the minds of some. A white man coming to the door of a farmhouse had a much better chance of receiving help. A Mexican would be automatically associated with the striking workers.

Word soon got out to transient people all over the state that pickings were slim in the five southern counties of the San Joaquin Valley, at least for the duration of this year's cotton strike. The irony of this situation was that it also limited the ability of local farmers to secure the services of homeless men as strike breakers.

As it turned out, Valley farmers had to advertise as far away as Texas in order to entice workers to their districts to serve as strike breakers. This act undoubtedly contributed to the western movement of the Dust Bowl victims of Oklahoma, Arkansas and Texas. Word was, there was work in California – go west young man, go west.

Jake continued talking to local merchants as the number of workers lingering around the Union Hall began to swell. Jake estimated that as many as 600 to 700 hundred workers filled the Hall and the surrounding street and sidewalks.

Pat Chambers and several of his lieutenants arrived to a cheer, and he moved among the workers, shaking hands and receiving pats on the back as he slowly worked his way to the building.

His presence seemed to electrify the situation. Jake was impressed at how such a soft-spoken man with an almost frail appearance could generate so much passion.

Chambers entered the building as the wake of workers closed around him and crowded into the stairwell. The primary meeting would take place on the second floor, although both floors were jammed with people who hoped to be as close to the event as possible.

Jake chose not to enter the building, although he had been invited. He decided that he could get whatever he needed about the content of the speech from Veronica. He felt that it would be the response of the people of Citrus Grove that would be the story.

As he hung around the grocery store, he talked to its owner, Jim Cole. Jake knew Jim to be a prudent man who knew on which side his bread was buttered, but he also was a square shooter. As a long time member of the community from a well established and influential family, Jim Cole was also not afraid of the farmers. He knew they could not touch him. His family name was one of the most recognized in the southern valley. He also had quite a bit of money, although he did not flaunt it, and he could fight back against anyone who might try to push him around. This is what Jake was banking on.

"What do you think about all of this Jim?" Jake asked as they stood on the sidewalk in front of the grocery store watching the swell of workers in front of the Hall.

"You know there are two sides to any question," he responded. "But let's face it, Jake. Most of these workers will be gone in a few of weeks. What do we really owe them?"

"But what do they do for your business while they're here?" Jake continued.

"I have to admit that my sales go up about 50 percent while they're in town," he said. "It is a nice boost every fall. But I would not fold up and blow away if they didn't return."

"But if they didn't return, what would happen to the farming industry in this county, and if the farmers failed, how would that affect your business?"

"In that case, I would have to leave too. There would be nothing left here to stay for. I guess when you put it that way, things could get pretty tough for everyone if local farmers had nobody to pick their crops."

"Do you think they know that?" Jake persisted.

"I am sure they do," Cole responded. "The problem is that I think they would rather see the town die than to give in to a bunch of Mexicans, but that is off the record."

At that moment, a commotion caught the attention of both men as a caravan of about a half dozen cars rumbled into the center of the street in a cloud of dust.

As the cars screeched to a stop in the middle of the street, men armed with guns and clubs jumped out of the doors and began to move toward the crowd.

Jake and the grocery store owner were out of earshot but close enough to clearly see the angry armed men as they shouted orders to members of the crowd.

Returning the shouts, male members of the crowd moved toward the front to meet the apparent threat, when, suddenly, something sparked a physical interchange between one of the armed men and a farm worker.

As the men exchanged blows, the armed men waded into the crowd waving shotguns, handguns and pick ax handles. Suddenly, some shots rang out, and screams from women in the crowd prompted a full scale retreat by women and children as men held a rear guard action to protect their retreating families by hurling rocks, bottles and anything else that could be found.

The armed men turned on the Union Hall and released a volley of shots that drove observers from the second story window back into the relative safety of the interior of the building.

In what seemed to be only a few seconds, several people lay sprawled on the ground among spent weapons cartridges, rocks and other debris as the armed men rushed back to their vehicles, piled in and drove away.

Jake and Jim Cole ran to the downed people to help, while others rushed out from the barbershop, shoe repair, pharmacy and various other businesses on the street in order to help the victims.

Several people were bleeding from head injuries as downtown merchants began to administer aid. Jake moved toward a woman who was screaming to discover that another woman was lying prostrate in the middle of the street, apparently shot in the abdomen, and from the looks of it more than once.

Another man was laying in the gutter in front of the Union Hall, obviously dead from a gunshot wound to the head. Jake stood still, continuing to look around, stunned by what he saw. The street looked like a war zone. There were broken windows in the Union Hall building, along with several bullet holes in the front wall.

The smell of gun smoke still filled the air. People stood in apparent shock and disbelief, while others ran for bandages and water to help the wounded. Dozens of those who had fled now returned to help. Many of those who had been in the building flooded into the street.

All of those injured appeared to be farm workers, while all of those who had started the fight disappeared apparently unscathed. Jake also noticed the obvious lack of police officers in the immediate area, and found that strange considering the fact that a union rally of this size had the potential for violence.

Several minutes would elapse before police authorities arrived. Some stayed to question the victims, while others left in an apparent hurry after the armed men.

Gordy appeared by Jake's side as he helped lift the wounded woman into a nearby car for transport to the County Hospital over in Gunderson. She was unconscious and unable to be of any help to the police.

Jake approached Gordy, visibly shaken by the events.

"Where the hell were you?" Jake asked Gordy in an accusatory tone. "You could have prevented this."

"Don't start on me, Jake. This isn't my fault."

"You knew about the rally. Why didn't you have some officers here?"

"Not now, Jake. I have work to do."

"There isn't going to be a cover-up Gordy," Jake said. "Not if I have anything to say about it."

Jake ran to the car he knew would be parked behind the diner and took it without asking, hoping to square it later with Barney. He roared out of town in the same direction that had the armed men had taken.

About fifteen minutes later he came across a group of Highway Patrolmen who had several men in custody. Jake pulled up and saw one police car with several guns in the trunk. He kicked himself that he didn't have his camera.

As near as he could figure, one of the cars of armed men had been stopped by a Highway Patrolman for speeding, which is when the guns were discovered. During questioning, several members of the pursuing sheriffs arrived, and the picture became clear.

At least five men were in custody, while intensive questioning revealed the names of several others who were on the run from the Citrus Grove riot. Jake noted their names, only to be turned away by police authorities. He knew at least one, and recognized three of the other four. All of them were either outright members of the Farmers Association or affiliated with it in some close way.

Realizing his presence would not be welcome by the sheriff's deputies, and knowing he could access the police reports later, Jake decided to return to town, reasonably satisfied that the rest of the men responsible for this disaster would probably be caught.

He made a detour to the hospital to find out about the female victim. When Jake arrived the hospital staff was very busy. He had no idea how many people had been killed or injured. The hospital was already overcrowded with beating victims on top of those who were suffering from malnutrition and dehydration from their striking activities. It was like the entire San Joaquin Valley had suddenly been invaded by a foreign army, and the casualties were mounting.

Jake inquired about the woman who had been shot and discovered that Dr. Joel McIntosh had been on duty when she arrived. Jake had met Dr. McIntosh when he was covering the story about the killing of the Delgado boy.

Finding the doctor, Jake asked how the woman was doing.

"She was dead on arrival," he said. "She bled to death from two bullet wounds to the abdomen. But even if she had arrived sooner, there probably wasn't anything we could have done. The damage was too great. Her insides were torn up pretty bad. "

"Do you know who she was?" Jake asked.

"She has been identified as Juanita Nunez. She was a resident of Corcoran."

"Have you got anything on the other shooting victim?"

"No," the doctor answered. "He was declared dead at the scene and taken to the morgue, and his identity isn't known at this time."

"What is happening around here?" the doctor asked. "I've never seen anything like this."

"There is a cotton strike on," Jake replied. "Haven't you heard?"

"Of course, but this is suppose to be a dispute over wages," McIntosh said, "not world war two."

"Maybe you should explain that to the Farmers Association," Jake said. "I wish I could stay and chat, but I have a lot of work to do. Thanks for the information."

Jake stopped off at the sheriff's office to see if he could get the names of the men who had been arrested, along with any other details about the incident.

Coincidentally, Gordy was in the front office. Jake approached with an ashamed look on his face.

"Hay Gordy," Jake said. "I'm sorry for the way I talked to you earlier. It was stupid."

"No need to apologize," Gordy answered. "Everyone is very upset these days. Listen, I have some paperwork I need to wrap up. How about if I meet you at the coffee shop across from the movie theater in about 15 minutes? And do me a favor. Keep this meeting between you and me."

"What's up?" Jake asked.

"I'll see you in about 15 minutes."

Jake left without saying another word. Gordy must have something big.

Jake was on his second cup of coffee when Gordy walked in the back door in civilian clothes. Gordy immediately sat down at Jake's table with his usual greeting.

"Hi Jake," he said. "Sorry for putting you off; I wanted to speak to you alone. But you can't use my name. It would probably cost me my job. I am not going to tell you anything you couldn't find out on your own eventually. I just don't want anyone to know you got it from me. I am just saving you some time.

"Well, you asked me on the street where we were. Sure, we knew about the rally, and three cars were ordered to patrol Citrus Grove and be as visible as possible. Unfortunately, the guys didn't take it seriously and were hanging around behind Barney's several blocks away drinking coffee. I know most of them, and they probably didn't care much if some of the workers got hurt. They don't have much sympathy for the strikers."

"Is it because they are Mexican?" Jake asked.

"That's part of it, but there is talk that the union has communist affiliation. There are a lot of people around here who don't like that."

"I can see that," Jake said, "but anyone who doesn't play the farmer's game is labeled a communist. It is getting to the point that everyone who doesn't think like a narrow segment of this community is a communist. What about the farmers who were arrested? Who were they?"

"Here is a list," Gordy said. "We arrested five men, and about 20 more were named. There is an investigation underway to determine who might have been directly involved in the shootings."

"I don't recognize many of the names here," Jake said. "but the name Phillip Hogan rings a bell."

"It should," Gordy said. "He is married to J.C. Osgood's sister."

"He is Osgood's brother-in-law!" Jake exclaimed.

"That's right. J.J.'s uncle by marriage."

"Was J.J. involved?" Jake asked.

"His name hasn't come up," Gordy answered. "My guess is that he won't be named."

"You don't think he was involved?"

"That isn't what I said."

"Are you guys seeking the other names on this list?"

"Yes, and you can quote me on this. The sheriff's office is looking for all these men for questioning. We consider them material witnesses, and if they do not come in on their own, I suspect that warrants will be issued for their arrest."

"Do you know any of these men?" Jake asked.

"Not personally, but they are all local men and are probably not going anywhere."

"Wow," Jake said. "This is unbelievable. I couldn't imagine this could happen here."

"This is off the record again, but I am not surprised. The talk around the station is that those Mexicans had it coming."

"I guess I have heard enough for now," Jake said. "I won't use your name, even where you said I could. I don't want to jeopardize your position. I'd better go, Gordy. Thanks for the help. The people have a right to know what's going on."

"I've heard that speech before Jake, but I didn't believe it until now. You leave first. I'll wait a few minutes before I leave."

Jake drove the 30 or so miles back to Citrus Grove. As he traveled he mulled the situation over in his mind. This was the biggest story he had ever covered. Was he doing the right thing? Was he losing his objectivity? But then, had he ever been objective?

In the past he seemed to spend a lot of time cheer leading for the people who were now part of this mess. Now, he seemed to be turning against them, even in his own mind. But wasn't it the responsibility of a journalist to report the facts? Wasn't it his responsibility to print the truth, even if it could cost him something?

He also began to wonder if he had been partly responsible for inflaming the situation. When he thought back to the comment made by the union organizer at the Woodville barn riot, "if that was all the farmer's had, the union had nothing to fear." Maybe it was inappropriate to print that quote. Obviously, it wasn't all the farmers' had. Maybe some farmers read that quote and decided to take it to the union. If that is so, did Jake play a role in this mess?

When Jake returned to Citrus Grove, his first step was to return the car to Barney. As it turned out, Barney was too sloshed to even notice the car was gone. Jake nevertheless thanked him for the use and promised to make it up to him.

Jake went straight to his office in order to get everything down for Friday's edition. It was going to be a busy couple of days.

Blood Flows in Downtown Citrus Grove, the headline read. *Five Farmers Arrested for the Gunshot Deaths of Two Mexican Farm Workers*, said the sub headline. There was no writer's block today. Jake was on a roll.

"At about noon on Tuesday two dozen well-armed men attacked a crowd of some 500 unarmed workers killing two and severely injuring scores of others," the article began.

"Phillip Hogan, William Stern, George Applebee, Harold Kitchens and Vincent O'Neil are being held at the county jail pending a preliminary hearing. A list of other suspects is currently in the hands of police officials, and further arrests are expected.

"Jim Cole, owner of Cole's Grocery, witnessed the event from the sidewalk in front of his Main Street store. 'I can't believe what I saw,' he said. 'People were being cut down like sheep. The place looked like a war zone.'

"During the melee, sheriff's deputies were nowhere to be found, despite the fact the union rally was well publicized and the two factions had clashed before.

"After the shooting was over, three carloads of sheriff's deputies, who had been hanging around behind Barney' Diner drinking coffee, arrived to find at least 30 people lying in the middle of the street or nursing various wounds.

"One unidentified man, about 35 years old, with a dark complexion and about five foot nine, was declared dead on the scene from a gunshot wound to the head. His body was transported to the county morgue, where it rests while awaiting the expected inquest and contacting the next of kin.

"A second victim, identified as Juanita Nunez, died on the way to the hospital, reportedly from two gunshot wounds to the abdomen."

Jake continued with the story, and with several other related stories about the escalating violence throughout the county.

He made sure to report the name of Phillip Hogan as one of those allegedly involved, which clearly implicated the Farmers Association and the town's most prominent citizen, J.C. Osgood.

Jake realized when he wrote the story that his neck was stuck out a long way. But he felt it was time to expose the farming corruption in this valley, and he knew more questionable information would be revealed in the days to come.

Jake was going to blow the lid off of this town, and his future was going to be in the hands of his readers. Would they stand up and support the truth? Or, would they side with the farmers as they always had?

Jake never expected to find himself in this position, and he could have avoided it. Maybe it was Veronica who had awakened in him his real self.

That was not all she had awakened in him.

Chapter Nine

It was the start of another week, and Jake Rogers hit the streets early this morning. His latest edition had been out for a couple of days, but he had kept a low profile over the weekend. Now that he was back in circulation, he expected to hear the fallout of this week's news coverage.

But he felt confident that the information in his most recent edition was accurate. The articles were tough and hard hitting, but they were the truth, at least as Jake saw it. The farmers would not accept any "truth" that portrayed them in anything but the best possible light. They had enjoyed years, and even generations, of press support. Even Jake had been part of that history. He had also seen what happened to newspapermen in other small towns who did not march lock step with the Farmers Association. Jake decided that he would rely on the sense of fairness of the general population, many of whom had been victimized by the big farmers as well.

Jake had by now made an agreement with Barney to use his car at will. It looked like his own car would never get fixed, and he may not be able to pay for it if it did.

He began the morning by driving to the county seat in Gunderson to look at the court agenda. He expected the men who were arrested for the Citrus Grove killings to be arraigned today. He also expected the county coroner to conduct an inquest about the killings. In both cases he was right. Notice of the inquest was posted in the hallway of the County Court building right next to the arraignment schedule. Luckily, they were planned several hours apart, so he would be able to attend them both.

He had about an hour before the arraignment, and the inquest would be this afternoon. That gave him plenty of time to look over the police reports more thoroughly. Jake also planned to keep on the lookout for Solomon Wirinski. He might or might not be actually involved in the arraignment and inquest. But he would undoubtedly be interested in the information.

Jake made his first stop the sheriff's department, where he hoped to interview some of the arresting officers involved in the Citrus Grove incident. But he was met with hostility after entering the building.

"Hello," Jake greeted the officer on the

desk. "I would like to view the official report on the Citrus Grove murders last week."

"Why?" the deputy snapped. "So you can write some more trash about us?"

"What's that suppose to mean?" Jake asked. "What was that crack you printed about our guys drinking coffee instead of doing their jobs?"

"Oh, that. News travels fast in Gunderson. That edition just hit the street in Citrus Grove, and we don't even circulate in this town."

"We got a copy of your rag before it was shipped. One of our deputies has a friend who works in the print shop at the Globe."

"Imagine that," Jake said sarcastically. "Small world."

"Well I am not going to let you in, smart ass," the deputy said. "How about that."

"You will let me in," Jake said. "It's called the First Amendment. Ever hear about it?"

"What's the trouble here?" another, obviously higher ranking deputy asked, overhearing the dispute.

"This jerk wants to see our log," the desk sergeant said.

"Let him in," the other deputy said. "He

has a right to his opinion. We don't have to like it."

"Thank you," Jake said. "I would like to see the police reports on the Citrus Grove killings."

The second deputy led Jake to a file room where he was left alone. The deputy pulled the folder containing the report and handed it to Jake.

"I can't control what you print," said the deputy, "but please do not print anything that could jeopardize our investigation."

"Fair enough," Jake said, "and thanks for your understanding."

"You have a job to do, and so do I. I think we can both do it better if we can get along," the officer said before turning and walking out the door.

Jake sat down at the table in the middle of the room and began to pour over the report.

Gordy had been very thorough. He had given Jake nearly everything, except for a few details. For instance, the guns found in the possession of those arrested were still smoking and the gun barrels were still warm according to the report. It was obvious to the officer that the guns had been fired within the last few minutes. The suspects readily admitted to being at the rally, but all denied possessing or using weapons. The guns in the trunk of the car had been used for hunting the day before, the suspects said. There was no question that the farmers were lying.

The suspects had been interrogated after their arrests, and more names of those involved had been revealed. This was information that Gordy did not have in his possession when he and Jake spoke at the coffee shop. The names would not do Jake much good at the moment, since his next edition would not be released for several days. Daily newspapers would publish the names, and warrants would probably be issued for their arrests from the court this morning. Weekly newspapers can't directly compete with dailies, since in a weekly format some of the news is several days old before the paper hits the street. Jake was wasting his time. He needed a different angle.

His next stop was the courthouse, where he would get his first view of the suspects. Normal procedure required their appearance in court during their arraignment.

The morning arraignment schedule wouldn't begin for about 20 minutes, so Jake hung around in the lobby just to see whatever he could see. Just as he was ready to enter the courtroom, in walked Solomon Wirinski. Jake met him at the courtroom door.

"Suppose we could talk after the arraignment?" Jake asked.

"Sure," Wirinski responded.

The two men strolled to the front row of seating. Both had by now begun to develop a respect for the other. Jake was put off by Wirinski at first because of his confrontational demeanor. But Jake now realized that a day in and day out battle against what Wirinski saw as evil forces probably had a great deal to do with Wirinski's attitude. He undoubtedly believed he was a candle of justice in the eye of a hurricane of political, social and economic corruption. At least that was Jake's assessment of the situation. And Jake was beginning to be sympathetic with Wirinski's point of view.

Wirinski at first looked upon Jake as just another sell-out with no ideals, putting his own welfare before the welfare of the community where he lived. Jake had to admit that Wirinski probably was justified in seeing Jake in this light. But there had been a noticeable change in Jake, and Wirinski had seen it in the articles he wrote. Jake seemed to be changing into the kind of man that Wirinski could admire, a sort of metamorphosis – a worm changing into a butterfly, so to speak.

Wirinski also knew that having an ally in the press was no small thing. The entire issue of justice for any management-labor dispute depended on where the public stood. It was the citizens of Citrus Grove who were the front line against corruption. In a dictatorship, power is taken, sometimes at the point of a gun. In a democracy, power can only be given freely. Public opinion is the final arbiter, and the press is the best tool for informing the public, which is why a dictator - in this case the farmers - will censor the press as a way of holding on to power.

The two men engaged in light conversation as they waited for the arraignment to begin. They talked about life, the news business and being an ACLU lawyer. The one thing they both realized about the other is the loneliness they both endured. Each man in his own way isolated himself from the world around him, Wirinski in his dream to change the world, and Jake in his desire to hide from it. Wirinski had come to understand that most people don't want change, even if it is for the best. And Jake seemed to be going through the motions, with no dreams, no goals, and nobody to give a damn whether he lived or died. Change had not seemed to be a word that Jake recognized, that is not until recently.

Suddenly, a bailiff entered the room from a side door and announced the arrival of the judge.

"All rise for the honorable Judge Oliver Reed," the bailiff ordered.

"Please be seated," he added once the judge had taken his place at the bench.

"Can we have the first case," Judge Reed boomed.

"The first matter is in people versus Phillip Hogan, William Stern, George Applebee, Harold Kitchens and Vincent O'Neil," the clerk said. "They are being held as material witnesses in the untimely deaths of Juanita Nunez and the as of yet unidentified man of apparent Spanish decent known only at this point as John Doe."

"Untimely deaths," Wirinski exclaimed to Jake in a low tone. "It's called murder where I come from. The whitewash has already started."

"These men are all upstanding members of the community your honor," said Jeffrey Lawrence, the defense attorney in the case. "There is no risk of flight. They all have very strong ties here, family, jobs, church. We believe it would be appropriate to release them on their own recognizance."

"Upstanding," Wirinski said sarcastically, again in a low tone as he leaned in Jake's direction. "If they represent the best this town has, I can't imagine how the lowlifes behave."

Jake couldn't help but chuckle at Wirinski's remark.

"Mr. Green the judge said.

"We believe that reasonable bail is appropriate," said Tulare County District Attorney George Green.

"I agree," the judge responded. "Bail is set at $1,000 each."

The judge banged his gavel.

"Next case," he said.

"Oh please," Wirinski said as he stood to leave.

"Is that it?" Jake asked.

"This stinks," Wirinski said. "Either that judge is incompetent, or he is in cahoots. If I understand it, those guys haven't even been formally charged yet. And they will be on the street in 20 minutes."

"What do you mean they haven't been charged?" Jake asked.

"Did you hear a plea?" Wirinski asked.

"Have you ever been to an arraignment where no charges were read and no plea entered? And what about that bail, $1,000? That's unheard of in a case like this. If I remember correctly, that is the going rate for Mexican vagrancy in this county."

"How can they get away with that?" Jake asked.

"There are no charges yet. That's how they get away with it. If the charge was murder, the bail would have to be much higher for appearance sake if nothing else. They will be charged later behind closed doors out of sight of public scrutiny, since that is going to save face for the district attorney. But they will be charged while they are already free, so the bail won't come under scrutiny, since it has already been established. That will save face for the judge.

And if you report on this, your ass will be in a sling. The judge, district attorney and Farmers Association all will begin looking for ways to discredit you at least, or at worst invite you to leave town on a rail. I have heard of cases where rabble rousers disappeared, supposedly last seen leaving town on the southbound bus, only to have their bodies turn up days or weeks later along a remote stretch of highway."

"It's a conspiracy!" Jake said. "But the general public doesn't know what is going on."

"Now you have got it," Wirinski responded. "You have just seen farmer justice in action. That is what I have been trying to tell you all along."

"I didn't understand," Jake said.

"Now do you understand?" Wirinski asked.

The question didn't need an answer.

"I have some work to do," Wirinski said. "I'll be in front of the judge after lunch for the arraignment for some more union organizers. I already know the outcome. They will get $1,000 bail like the last group, the same you get for the murder of Mexican people if you are a farmer in this town. These union guys also have been in jail for several days. Not only do they have separate justice than the farmers, but it is slower in coming."

"I've got things to do, too," Jake said. "Will I see you at the inquest this afternoon?"

"Yes, I will be there," Wirinski responded, and the two went their separate ways.

Jake had some time to kill, so he decided to go over to the Gunderson Globe where his newspaper was printed. The Globe was also the largest daily newspaper in the county. As a consequence, it also had the largest printing press, and he had several acquaintances there.

Jake walked to the front desk and asked for the editor, Mitchell Hurley. Jake had known Hurley for years, and they had not had the chance to sit down and talk for months.

"Jake," Hurley said. "Long time no see. Come on in…. Have a seat…. I have watched your coverage of this strike. You sure are hitting the farmers where they hurt."

"I'm just printing the news," Jake responded. "Where does the Globe stand on the issue?"

"Well, the union is communist backed. We know that much. And the workers are migrants, so they will be gone in a few weeks. The farmers are our people. The choice on who to support is obvious. I find it hard to believe you don't see that. The tone of your coverage sounds almost like you are one of them.

"I've known you for a long time, Jake. I knew the previous owner of your newspaper. He was a good man. I wonder what he would think about his newspaper now. I'll bet he wouldn't agree with the approach you seem to be taking."

"I came here to see an old friend, Mitch, not to get a lecture. You have been in this business a long time. Why does this newspaper bend to the farmers' will? They don't have as much leverage on you as they do on me. Why doesn't the Globe print the facts instead of catering to the farming industry?"

"Now who's lecturing, Jake? We have our way of doing things. The farmers support this county. They are our people. Those Mexicans are foreigners. Let them make their wages and then go back to where they belong."

"California used to belong to Mexico, Mitch. Or have you forgotten that."

"No, I haven't forgotten. But what did they do with it. It was nothing until the United States got it. It was mostly populated with savages when the Americans arrived. We built this country. Now it belongs to us, and I for one don't want to see a bunch of Mexicans overrun us. Let them get their wages and go back to Mexico where they belong. I like the cheap tomatoes they give me, but that doesn't mean I want them living next door to me."

Just then the phone rang, and Hurley was tied up for several minutes. Jake sat in silence as he thought about what his old friend had said. Those sentiments were common. When Jake talked of these issues with the Delgados and others who lived in the Mexican part of Citrus Grove, the story was different.

In fact, Jake remembered a similar conversation he had with Senor Delgado just the other day.

"My ancestors invited the Americans into Texas to be friends and to help us build a Mexican state. But they stabbed us in the back and stole the territory away from us. They promised to respect our ways, but they didn't mean it. The same thing happened in California. We respected the Americans and allowed them to live among us. But as soon as they grew in numbers, they took California too. And after they took control of the government, they robbed us of our property and stripped us of our dignity. This cotton dispute is not about money," Delgado said. "It is about fear. They fear we will come in great numbers and take the land back and do to them what they did to us."

"Sorry," Hurley said, breaking Jake out of his daydream. "What were we saying?"

"Nothing much," Jake responded. "I think I'll be going. There is an inquest this afternoon on the Citrus Grove murders, and I have some things to do."

"Murders!" Hurley exclaimed. "It was self defense. In fact, their lawyer said he was going to enter a plea of self-defense. It's cut and dry. I don't understand why they are going to even have a trial."

"Two unarmed people were gunned down in the middle of the street in broad daylight. I call that murder," Jake said.

"I'd stay away from that kind of talk," Hurley said. "You push that thinking too far, and you're going to get yourself into trouble."

"Thanks for the advise," Jake said as he rose to leave.

"They're all in this together," Jake thought. "How could I have been so stupid?"

Jake arrived at the courthouse, where the inquest was scheduled to begin at 3 p.m. He hung around for about an hour watching the people come and go. His experience with the law was limited, since he had spent most of his time writing articles about social events in his home town, fund raisers, scholarship awards at the local high school, and other similar activities.

The one time he tried to enter into the police arena was when he published the police log of arrests for one Saturday night. The backlash was enormous. As it turned out, a couple of the town's "upstanding" citizens had been hauled in for being drunk in public. Not only did their families complain about Jake's coverage, but others in the community who feared the same thing happening to them wrote scathing letters to the editor.

"It is not the function of a community newspaper to pry into the personal lives the citizens living in that community," one letter said. "When a newspaper becomes a peeping Tom, it no longer serves the community."

Of course, peeping into the lives of the less fortunate on the poor side of town was not only acceptable but expected, since the bad press tended to justify the bigotry of white community members, at least, so they thought.

The bottom line of Jake's apparent lapse of journalistic judgment was that his advertising support dropped off for about a month, and Jake was in a severe pinch. He got the message real quick. Even when he tried to report on legitimate stories, like the Delgado boy killing, or the barn that J.J. burnt down, there were still problems. Jake tried to keep out of the legal arena after that. But what had it cost him? Now, he felt that he hadn't been doing his job, that he had exhibited no principles, no integrity. But it was never too late to change.

The time for the inquest had arrived, and Jake moved into the courtroom to the front row, which was his custom. The proceedings began, but with much more interest in this issue than normal. Usually, a county inquest was for an unusual death, like suicide.

Jake remembered back to a time when a beloved member of the community had killed himself. He was a retired school teacher who had taught social science at the high school, and coached baseball for years. When the team won the regional championship, the town gave him a parade.

His wife had died and he was suffering from terminal cancer. Out of despair, he put the barrel of a shotgun in his mouth and blew the back of his head off. Jake had not reported the incident out of respect, but then again he didn't need to because everyone in town knew what had happened within hours of the incident.

Sure, there had been times in the past where an inquest was held for murders, but never under these circumstances, where prominent members of the community were the ones being accused of the crime. Usually the story centered on the discovery of the body of a migrant worker who few people cared about. In these cases, community members expected to hear all of the sordid details of the death in their newspaper.

The public record on the cause of death was read allowed by the county clerk.

"Regarding the death of the as yet unidentified man, a medical examination revealed that he was shot at close range in the left temple by a .22 caliber pistol.

"The conclusion of the medical examiner is that the impact of the bullet caused the head to recoil, turning it three inches to the right before a second bullet entered the victim's head behind his left ear.

"The lack of bleeding causes the medical examiner to conclude that death was instantaneous. The man was probably was dead before he hit the ground.

"There was no skin under the finger nails and no bruises that would reflect any defensive activity on the part of the victim toward his assailant. The conclusion by the medical examiner is that the victim probably did not know he was about to be shot.

"Regarding the death of Juanita Nunez,"

the clerk continued, "the medical examination shows that the victim was shot in the abdomen at close range with a .38 caliber bullet.

"The examination also showed that she had gun powder residue on her left wrist and inside arm in a pattern density that suggests she had a hold of the gun barrel when it was fired.

"The conclusion is that she tried to prevent the assailant from shooting her by grabbing the gun in an apparent attempt to push the gun aside as it went off. Further examination shows that a second .38 caliber bullet entered her body just below the sternum while she was prostrate on the ground. The conclusion by the medical examiner is that the assailant was standing above her and shot downward into her body as she lay on her back.

"Mrs. Nunez died of massive bleeding as a result of the gun shot wounds."

After several minutes of public discussion about the findings on the cause of death, the county coroner concluded that the deceased died "at the hands of persons unknown." This comment prompted several members of the gallery to jump to their feet in public outrage. One man in the audience yelled the sentiments of most of the other farm workers who were present.

"Everyone knows damn well who killed those people!" he said in a vocal octave well above the rest of the commotion. "The coroner's office is just another tool of the farmers."

Jake turned to see who was doing the yelling, and struggled to see over the crowd of farm workers. Jake saw Solomon Wirinski standing at the back of the room behind the last row of seats. He should not have been surprised at Wirinski's outburst. He must have been among the last to arrive, which would explain why he was standing in the back. By the time the inquest had started, there was not a single empty seat.

Suddenly, a scuffle ensued, and Jake found himself being swept up in a flood of bodies moving toward the double door entrance to the room. In the confusion, Jake saw a couple of men attack Wirinski and drive him to the floor just about the time that several farm workers came to his rescue. The two assailants fought their way out of the doors and ran down the hall to the main entrance, with at least 10 farm workers in pursuit.

Jake struggled through the crowd to

Wirinski's location on the floor. By then, he was already sitting up nursing a bloody nose.

"Quite exhilarating!" Wirinski exclaimed with a broad smile on his face. "I guess I hit a soft spot."

Jake stood over Wirinski, smiling down on him with his hands on his hips.

"I think you are enjoying this," Jake said.

"I have been called a lot of names, but this is the first blood I have given for the cause. I guess it's part of the price you pay for voicing an unpopular opinion around here."

"Come on Sol, let's get you a cup of coffee," Jake said as he helped Wirinski to his feet.

The two men spent the rest of the day together, laughing about the scuffle and talking about the strike. Jake began to form a great admiration for his newfound friend.

"It's getting late," Wirinski said. "I've got a big day tomorrow."

"Me too," Jake responded, "and I have to get Barney's car back to him."

Jake drove back to Citrus Grove to return the car, and found himself not wanting to return to his dilapidated apartment. It had never seemed so, but for some reason his whole life now seemed dreary, his job, his apartment, his world. When this was all over, maybe he would find a dream and chase after it.

He decided to go over to the Mexican side of town, where he knew he could find people who would not judge him or his actions. He did not have to live up to anyone's expectations over there. People tended to accept you at face value, without pretensions. He walked toward La Cantina del Sol, and as he approached the front he seemed to hear a cold one calling his name from inside. He went in, sat down on a stool at the bar and ordered a beer. It had been a long day.

Chapter Ten

Jake Rogers had trouble getting out of bed this morning. His little stint at the local bar had gone farther than he had planned, and he needed some time to recover. The coffee was on, and he dressed. The day was warming up as usual, and Jake decided to go downstairs to his office and browse the out of town newspapers to begin the day. The strike had become state news. Both the San Francisco Chronicle and Los Angeles Times had representatives in the Valley looking for news items to be publish in their newspapers. The Sacramento and San Jose newspapers were also picking up stories on the strike.

The strike had produced a lot of news. The Times reported that in five southern San Joaquin Valley counties, as many as 25,000 workers had walked out. In some areas, cotton picking had virtually stopped. Workers who had not joined the strike were now being targeted by strikers as scabs, a derogatory name used to describe people who worked while their brethren struck for better wages. Out-of-state recruiting activities by San Joaquin Valley farmers were beginning to pay off. A flood of destitute white families were pouring into the area from as far away as Texas and Oklahoma, overwhelming city and county services wherever they settled.

The arrival of the white workers from the Dust Bowl also resulted in racial violence between the workers. Farmers were using the new arrivals as strike breakers.

Reports of worker-worker violence undoubtedly undermined the union cause while it bolstered the cause of the Farmers Association. The violence had escalated to the point that public outcry for the National Guard to be sent in had become almost common place.

According to the San Francisco Chronicle, even the United States Department of Justice introduced an additional complication when it threatened to send in police support. As it turned out, the man who was murdered in the Citrus Grove incident had been identified as Rogelio Roblero, a member of the Mexican Consulate staff in Monterey. He had been sent in to investigate reports that Mexican nationals were among those under arrest. His murder prompted an official complaint by the Mexican Government, and the Justice Department was ordered by President Roosevelt to intervene if

California didn't take steps to stop the violence.

California Governor John Rolph, after a significant period of apparent apathy, finally consented to send in an estimated 100 California Highway Patrol officers to help the besieged southern San Joaquin Valley.

The Sacramento Bee reported that under increasing political pressure, the Governor appointed several men from around the state to form a mediation committee that was to arrive in Citrus Grove within a few days. Citrus Grove had been chosen as the site of the mediation process because it was the location that seemed to be the center of the dispute.

The committee was to be made up of agriculture professionals and labor experts. The governor even appointed an economics professor from Stanford University to sit on the committee. This was the first ray of hope to hit the Southern Valley since the strike began. Something would have to happen soon, however, since the jails were overflowing and the county court system was severely gridlocked.

Jake continued to review news items until the morning was gone. He realized that the day was slipping away, so he decided to go out to the Corcoran refugee camp to see how they were doing. Maybe things had settled down enough for camp residents to live in peace.

Traveling in Barney's car was an experience that everyone needed to have at least once in his lifetime. Nearly every joint rattled as the car rumbled along the road. Rust had nearly eaten through the car body in several spots, which illustrated severe neglect – particularly when one considers that the valley climate is generally not conducive to body rust. A car owner in the valley has to almost work at getting his car to rust like Barney's had.

The drive did not interfere with Jake's appreciation of the view, however. He had been in this valley for a long time. Where many others viewed the valley as barren, almost desert like, he was able to see a beautiful side. Sure, there were times when he suffered from the heat like everyone else. But the spring could be very pleasant. And he loved the infrequent storms that blew the dust away, leaving behind clear air and abundant wildflowers. The valley could be very beautiful, he thought.

He arrived at the camp and immediately

saw several improvements. The union had hauled in a larger water tank which was undoubtedly capable of holding hundreds of gallons of fresh water. As he entered the camp, he also noted that the smell had receded quite a bit. In addition, there were no guards at the entrance – a good sign. Maybe things were looking up.

He drove around the camp for several minutes, until he came to a campsite that seemed to be different than the rest. It was more organized. It also had a large tent that was apparently used as a meeting place.

Jake parked his car and approached the campsite and was pleasantly surprised to discover that Veronica was standing with a group of union men who were engaged in a serious discussion. He walked toward the group in order to overhear what was being said.

"He's one of the few friends we have," one man said. "We've got to do something."

"Yea," said another, "let's organize a search party."

As Jake approached the gathering, Veronica spotted him and ran to his side.

"What's going on?" he asked.

"Mr. Wirinski is missing," she said. "He

left here last night, and he never made it back to his hotel."

"You're kidding," Jake said. "What could have happened?"

"Pat believes it might be connected to the scuffle at the inquest yesterday. There has been a lot of bad talk among the farmers about his presence. They feel he is an outsider coming in to stir up trouble. We're afraid something could have happened to him."

"I'm going to look for him," Jake said. "Will you come with me?"

"Of course," Veronica responded.

"Pat, we're going to see if we can find Sol," Jake said. "I'm going to see if I can retrace his route to Citrus Grove."

"We're right behind you," Chambers responded, "as soon as we can get organized."

Jake and Veronica cruised the obvious routes that Solomon Wirinski might have taken, ending their search at the hotel where he had been staying. The desk clerk knew him as a result of several days of interaction while the lawyer came and went about his business. The clerk said that he had not seen Wirinski since early morning the previous day.

Jake voiced concern about his friend and prevailed upon the desk clerk to let him into

Wirinski's room. The desk clerk balked, citing a hotel policy about privacy.

"Look," Jake said, "Something might be very wrong here. You can come with us if you like."

Recognizing the seriousness of the situation, the clerk gave Jake the key to Wirinski's room.

Jake and Veronica entered the room.

"Everything seems okay here," Jake said. "Clothes are hung in the closet. I'll check the bathroom."

"His dresser seems okay," Veronica added, "and his bed is made."

"Let's go," Jake said. "He's got to be around somewhere."

Jake and Veronica continued their search along less well traveled roads around the county, trying to think of anyplace he might be. Chambers has dispatched union people to the hospitals and jails. Even the morgue was checked. Every time one searcher came into contact with another, they exchanged whatever information they had. By now the search party numbered into the dozens.

The day wore on.

"Maybe he was suddenly called back to Los Angeles by his office," Veronica said in obvious desperation.

"I doubt it," Jake said. "He would have left word with someone, even if it was only with the desk clerk. Besides, his tooth brush was still in the bathroom. No, something must have happened. He wasn't planning to go anywhere."

"I was afraid you would say that," Veronica said. "He must be hurt."

The pair searched as the hours slipped by. At one point, they ran into Pat Chambers in another automobile and stopped to better coordinate the search.

"I called his office," Chambers said. "Wirinski hasn't called in for two days. They say that he calls in nearly every morning to check in and get his messages. They fear the worst."

The group went about their search with a renewed sense of urgency. Daylight was fading, and Jake knew that if his friend was hurt, another night outside without some help might be his last.

Jake retraced his search back toward the camp, and on a whim slowed his vehicle to a crawl just outside of sight of the place where he was last seen.

Suddenly, Veronica yelled.

"Stop Jake. I see something."

Jake pulled off the road onto the dirt, and the two got out of the car.

"Look over there," she said. "It looks like a car swerved into those almond trees."

Jake rushed to the spot and verified Veronica's observation."

"Good girl," Jake said. "I think we're on to something."

Jake looked at the ground, walked around and looked some more.

"It looks like three or four cars were here," he said. "I can see at least that many tire marks. They seem to go back into that row of trees. Let's go."

Jake and Veronica rushed back to the car, and Jake spared no time getting on the trail. Jake drove the car between rows of trees for nearly a hundred yards, until he saw what appeared to be an abandoned car.

"There's his car," Jake said excitedly.

He screeched to a halt and Veronica bolted out of her side and ran to what it looked like could be a body lying about thirty feet from the abandoned car. Jake yelled to her to be careful, but she disregarded his warning.

"Jake! It's Mr. Wirinski."

Jake rushed to her side and pulled

Wirinski onto his lap.

"Is he alive," Veronica said, her eyes welling up with tears.

"Yes, but he's in bad shape. Help me get him to the car."

Jake and Veronica gently lifted the man and laid him in the back seat of the car. His face was badly beaten, and he appeared to have other wounds. Jake had no medical knowledge, so he did not try to render aid, believing that no time should be lost in getting Wirinski to the hospital.

Jake drove as fast as he could, but the hospital was 30 minutes away. His mind swirled as he feared for his friend's health. But the time passed quickly, and they were at the hospital in no time.

"Help me get him inside."

Veronica had stayed in the back seat with the injured man, trying to comfort him as much as possible. He even seemed to be coming around a little by the time they reached their destination.

A medial staff member took Jake's friend and rushed him into an emergency area, and an attendant asked Jake and Veronica to wait.

"We will let you know his condition as

soon as he is examined," he said.

It was not more than 15 minutes when the attendant came out of the emergency area.

"Your friend has broken ribs, a broken nose and a severe head injury, not to mention many bruises and contusions. He has been badly beaten."

"Is he going to be all right?" Jake asked.

"He is going to recover, but that head injury may impair him for some time. He could have some long lasting motor problems. His speech may also be affected."

"Oh Jake!" Veronica said as she tightly embraced his arm.

The attendant left the two to their grief.

"He'll be okay," Jake said without confidence in his voice. "We can't do anything more tonight. Let's go back to town."

By now it was just after dark, and the valley breeze began to cool things down. Their drive was nearly in silence, both lost in their individual thoughts. As they approached Citrus Grove, Jake suggested the two go to La Cantina del Sol for a beer. Veronica agreed.

The couple entered the cantina and sought some seclusion at an out of the way booth. Neither of them felt the desire to socialize with others, and both suspected they could run into acquaintances. Ignacio, the bartender, saw them enter the building and sit down. He came to them to ask for their orders. Ignacio new both of them and approached with a broad smile on his face.

Both people were highly regarded in the Mexican community, but it was uncharacteristic by community standards that they would be seen together in a public place of this kind. Eyebrows would be raised in the white community if this pair was seen in an apparent social situation on the other side of town. Rumors would run wild. But she would never go there after dark, so the problem would never arise.

Jake ordered two beers, and Veronica acknowledged her consent.

"It's been a hard day," Jake said. "I hope Sol is all right."

"He is both a brave and a foolish man," Veronica said. "He fights for an unpopular cause knowing he is putting himself in danger. That takes courage, but I can't help wonder what he hopes to gain."

"He is not interested in personal gain," Jake said. "He fights because he believes in justice."

Ignacio arrived with two beers.

"Thanks," Jake said.

The pair resumed their conversation.

"What happens now?" Veronica asked.

"Newspapers are reporting that the governor is sending in state police, and he is organizing a mediation committee. That is a good sign."

"It has taken him a long time to take notice," she said. "If the man killed in the riot had not been a representative of the Mexican Government, the governor would not have acted. He would not take any political risks to save a bunch of Mexican field workers."

"What about you, Jake?" she asked. "You saw Mr. Wirinski. That could happen to you."

"I have thought of that," he said. "But I know too many people around here. They might put up with that kind of thing being done to an outsider. But I am too close to home. I don't think these guys will do that to me."

"Can you count on that?" she asked. "These people are capable of anything. The murders should have taught you that."

"You don't need to be concerned," he said.

"But I am. I don't want to see anything happen to you."

Jake looked at her with a great deal of affection, and she looked away in embarrassment.

"Maybe I shouldn't talk like that," she said.

All of a sudden there was nothing left to say. Jake suggested that he take her home. She agreed, and Jake went to the bar to pay Ignacio. As they left the Cantina, Jake opened the door for her, asking where she would be going. She gave him directions to a friend's house where several workers were staying, and they pulled up outside of the house.

Jake walked her to the door.

"When will I see you again?" he asked.

"I will let you know when we have the next rally," she said.

"That's not what I mean."

They looked at each other for several seconds, and Jake leaned down to kiss her. She met his kiss willingly, standing on her tip toes and wrapping her around his waist.

"I don't know if it can be this way between us," she said after they separated. "We live in different worlds. I would not be accepted in yours, and you would be crazy to give up what you have and try to live in mine."

He looked at her and realized she could

be speaking the truth.

"Let me know when there is another rally," he said.

"I will."

He walked to the car. He was a thinker, and his mind wander as he drove home.

On the way home he remembered his childhood and the talks he had with his mother. Mixing the races in the San Joaquin Valley in 1933 was still considered socially unacceptable. Jake also knew that organizations like the Ku Klux Klan were making a comeback in the Valley, and Ku Klux Klanners viewed race mixing as much more than socially unacceptable. They liked to use the bible to promote the idea that race mixing was against God's law.

If a Klu Klux Klanner were to see a black man even walking down a public street with a white woman, the black man's life would be in danger. He would literally be taking his life in his hands, not that there was a black man in the Valley dumb enough to do it.

The white woman would have an out: she simply could say that he forced her, and she would be excused.

After the release of the film "Birth of a Nation," perhaps the most controversial motion picture in American history, a resurgent fear -- dating back to the Civil War -- of white society was that the big, bad, black man was out to violate virtuous, white womanhood. The film was released in 1915, less than a generation before the San Joaquin Valley strike, and the KKK had made a dramatic comeback partly as a result of that film.

The film not only sent a chill through white America, but it seemed to legitimize the activities of the KKK as the only way to fight against the rising tide of non-whites. In addition, many of the newcomers to the Valley were from Oklahoma, Texas and Arkansas. These people from the Dust Bowl tended to bring their racial hatreds with them, hatred that carried over from as far back as the Civil War. Many of them had never even seen a Mexican, but if you were non-white, Jewish or a "Papist," their name for a Catholic, you were a target of their bigotry.

Europeans arriving in New York City also suffered as a result of this film. Both Italian Catholics and Jews poured into eastern American cities during the 1930s to escape fascism and Nazism. Too many so-called nativists of the eastern cities, these unwanted newcomers fared little better than the black people of the Jim Crow South.

Jake snapped back to reality. His brief daydream over. He had more pressing issues to occupy his mind.

Maybe he was kidding himself. He and Veronica would be accepted in the Mexican community, but how would he make a living. He remembered his parents' experiences. He would have to keep his newspaper business in order to survive. It was all he knew how to do. The problem was that his business would probably dry up once his advertisers realized he was spending his time with a Mexican woman. It was unlikely they could have a future together. He decided to put his personal problems aside for now.

Call Me Juan

Chapter Eleven

The next few days were fairly calm, probably because the mediation team had arrived, and both sides were optimistic that the strike would be settled and things would return to normal.

Some of the smaller farmers had already negotiated separately with their workers in order to get back to the harvest. They were concerned that the weather might drive them out of business altogether. All it took was one, big rain, and an entire season's harvest could be lost. A few of the farmers who had everything they owned in the harvest were getting nervous.

Some caved in for economic reasons, others because they too had been victimized by the big growers and were not part of the Farmers Association. Some of the smaller farmers saw the Association in the same light as did the workers, that they were a bunch of bullies who used their money and political connections not only to deny the workers a fair day's pay but to drive smaller farmers out of business as well.

Strikers also had their problems.

Malnutrition had become epidemic. Even though the workers never had much during the best of times, now many of them faced near starvation. Workers were anxious to go back to work at any wage. The focus of the attention was on the Farmers Association, who was the last holdout. Their critics said they could afford to hold out, small farmers could not.

Another reason for the apparent lull in the dispute was the fact that nearly all of the union organizers were in jail, including Pat Chambers. Chambers had been arrested on a charge of criminal syndicalism, a relatively new law that was meant to curb the activities of "subversives." The Criminal Syndicalism Law was used to rob people viewed as un-American of their civil rights. Subversives were usually defined as anyone who had the audacity to challenge the power structure. Typically, unions fit that definition.

The Tulare County District Attorney concluded that the union was responsible for the riot in Citrus Grove, where the field workers were killed, which seemed to justify the arrest of as many union people as possible. Jake began to believe that the arrests of union leaders was an illegal maneuver to help the farmers who were under arrest for the killings to avoid conviction. Blaming the incident on the union would play well to a jury when the men accused of the killings went to trial. It wouldn't hurt the district attorney's chances of re-election either.

The mediation team took a couple of days to get organized. Team members were given a series of complaints by both sides. It was up to the mediators to organize an agenda that would directly address the problems and lead to a solution.

One of the problems was that representatives of the Farmers Association stated that they would not negotiate with "a bunch of communists." So it took the better part of a day just to agree on who would be at the mediation hearing and how it would work.

It was decided that Committee Chairman Alvin Crutchfield would ask questions that would hopefully provide the committee with enough information to make a recommendation for a compromise. Each side would be also given the opportunity to ask questions. In other words, no direct negotiations between the farmers and workers would take place.

Another problem turned out to be how

to decide who would be acceptable to the other side to ask the questions. Solomon Wirinski wasn't available, since he was still recovering in the hospital. Union members said that Pat Chambers needed to be there, but the judge assigned to the Chamber's case would not let him out of jail to attend the hearings.

It was finally decided that the union secretary was the only person who knew enough about the demands and the problems of the workers to represent them in the absence of the others. The union would be represented by the CAWIU secretary, while the farmers had some of the best legal representation available in the Valley – advantage farmers.

Nevertheless, strikers felt they had at least a chance. The hope was that an independent mediation committee with no affiliation to either side would see the problems as they were and decide in favor of the workers. They were the exploited, and the farmers were the exploiters; anyone could see that, or so the strikers hoped.

The committee heard three days of testimony about wages, housing and legal intimidation. The workers said, for instance, that they could not get fair treatment as long as the sheriff's department swore in "special deputies," who were in reality farmers with a legal sanction to use their guns.

Carol Singleton, the CAWIU secretary, proved to be considerably more adept at the mediation process than the farmers had given her credit. She turned the tables on them more than once, and impressed the mediation committee with her aggressiveness. During one session, a Lt. Homer Fitzgerald was called in to testify about accusations of police brutality. Carol Singleton was given the opportunity to question him.

He was sworn in, and the committee let her have the floor.

"What is the justification for giving farmers the authority to arrest strikers?" she asked.

"The workers are causing too much trouble," he said. "We don't have enough manpower to deal with it. It is not unusual for us to take on special deputies in times of crisis."

"But most of the strikers are being arrested by these special deputies for trespassing despite the fact they are congregating on public roads," Singleton continued. "If they are not crossing onto private property, how can they be arrested for trespassing?"

"I am afraid you have your facts wrong," the Lieutenant responded. "Your people are breaking a whole host of local laws and ordinances."

"Farmers are behaving the same way as the strikers, but only workers are being arrested by these so-called special farmer deputies. Why don't you deputize some of the workers?" she asked. "We have a lot of upstanding citizens in this community who are workers."

Lt. Fitzgerald got mad at the question.

"Farmers are our people," he said. "The Mexican workers are dirty; we herd them like pigs!"

Farmers in the audience burst into laughter, while workers yelled their disapproval.

"You see!" Singleton remarked as she turned toward the committee. "We can't negotiate fairly in this kind of atmosphere."

At that point, one of the lawyers for the Farmers Association stepped up and addressed the committee.

"This is irrelevant," he said. "I thought we were here to discuss a wage settlement."

"Please sit down," Chairman Crutchfield

said. "We are trying to get the big picture."

During another session, both sides had the opportunity to testify about the conditions that the workers lived and worked in. Farmers argued that one of the reasons the pay seemed low was that the land owners provided their workers with housing free of charge as part of the wage compensation package.

However, it was common knowledge that the houses provided to the workers were little more than shacks. The dwellings did not have running water, electricity and in many cases did not even have glass in the windows.

Responding to the criticism of poor company housing, farmers said that workers had the option of living anywhere they liked, and that if they didn't like the company housing that was provided to them they should seek housing elsewhere.

The union argued that the wage paid to workers was not enough to support a decent place to live. In most cases, workers lived eight or ten to a room, if a vacant room could be found. Community members with an extra room occasionally rented to a worker, but only in the case where the worker was very well known and had excellent references, and only then if he were white. And the room was usually a tack room or something like that. Seldom were these accommodations much better than the company housing. It would be unheard of for white people to rent out a room in their homes to Mexican migrant workers.

Some homeowners in the Mexican part of town could bring in a little extra cash by renting out a room. But then there was a problem of transportation to the fields. Most workers did not have cars.

Local hotels seldom rented to Mexican workers at all, and if they did the prices were heavily inflated.

Occasionally, farmers rented tents to their workers, the cost of which would be deducted from the wages. Farmers were also known to deduct the provision of water from the wages of their workers. And, seldom did farmers provide toilet facilities in the fields. It was common for both men and women to be forced to relieve themselves in the nearest ditch.

In many cases, workers simply lived in their cars, or along side of the road. In one instance, a newspaper report said that workers in the Salinas area were living in caves carved out of the sides of hills. For the few farmers that had housing available for their workers, the conditions were worse than barns. Jake had even overheard farmers joke that they would not house their livestock in the buildings provided to their workers.

A prominent farmer was called in front of the committee to address the situation.

"Let me ask you one question," Singleton said, "would you live in company housing?"

The farmer answered no, which was the truth. But he was caught off guard with the question. The wily secretary asked him before he was fully settled into his chair. Consequently, he answered before he realized the implication of the question.

"You have no right to ask me something like that," he said indignantly. "We do the best we can. Our lives are not rosy either. We are suffering too. In case you haven't noticed, there is a depression on."

"Yes," Singleton countered, "but our people live this way all the time. The Depression hasn't changed anything for us. When the depression is over, you will return to your success; we will simply continue to suffer. Your children go to school. You have decent roofs over your heads, and food to eat.

You have proper medical care. We have none of those things. I haven't seen any farmers living in their cars or in their groves. Have you?"

"Mr. Chairman," a Farmer Association lawyer broke in, "this isn't getting us anywhere."

She is really making a show of this, Jake thought. The workers are in good hands, even if their top guns are out of the way.

Jake had heard all of this before, so he decided to leave the hearings and see how his friend was doing in the hospital. When he arrived, Wirinski was finishing his lunch.

"Hi Sol," Jake said. "How are they treating you?"

Wirinski perked up at the entrance of his friend.

"Hospital food," Wirinski answered. "You know how it is."

"You look terrible," Jake said. "How do you feel?"

"Pretty good, considering. I think they will let me out in a couple of days. But I will be returning to Los Angeles for a few weeks of rehabilitation. The ACLU has arranged for me to see a specialist. They say my motor skills will be slow in coming back. I took a big hit to the head."

"Can you identify any of them?" Jake asked.

"No, all I remember is that three cars forced me off of the road. A couple of guys drug me out of the car, and a big fellow began beating on me. It was dark."

"A big guy?" Jake asked. "Could it have been John Jr.?"

"I don't know," Wirinski said. "Someone hit me on the head, and everything was blurry after that. They're not playing games."

"Have the police interviewed you?" Jake asked.

"No. They don't care. As far as they are concerned, I am just another communist. And they will be glad to get rid of me. The farmers did them a favor."

"Well, I'll be looking into this, Sol. I won't let it pass."

"Don't waste your time, Jake. Even if you find out who is responsible, the police won't do anything about it. If their farmers can get away with murder, what makes you think the police will do anything about this?"

"What makes you think those farmers will go free?" Jake asked.

"Jake, you will forever be naïve about

this, won't you? The deck is stacked. The trial will be a dog and pony show."

"Not if I can help it," Jake said.

Wirinski seemed to be getting tired.

"Well, I guess I had better go, Sol. Is there anything I can do for you? Can I get you anything?"

"No, I am fine. But thanks."

"Take care, Sol. I'll try to get back by soon."

Jake left the hospital determined to find out who had beaten his friend, but he knew it wasn't going to be easy. Very few people would be willing to help, at least those who could help.

The mediation hearing lasted for nearly a week, and the committee was nearing a decision. Jake decided to be at the hearing at the conclusion. So did half the town.

The American Legion Hall, where the hearing took place, was able to hold about three hundred people. And not only was there standing room only, but many more who could not crowd into the building stood on the outside steps and out into the street.

The last crowd of this size to gather in town proved to be disastrous, with two deaths and many injured during a riot. Police officials would be on hand this time, however, and workers said it was because a significant number of the people in attendance were white and part of the power structure.

"The police wouldn't be here if we were all Mexican," one bystander told Jake. "They would like nothing more than for us to kill each other off if we wanted, and they wouldn't to a thing about it."

The committee met to announce its decision, and the audience began to quiet as the committee members took their places on the panel of tables and chairs on the elevated stage at the front of the room. Committee Chairman Alvin Crutchfield gaveled the crowd into silence and announced the hearing to order. The announcement was brief and to the point.

"The governor appointed state mediation committee has reviewed the circumstances that bring us here today and have the following, non-binding recommendations."

At the announcement that the decision was non-binding, a roar emanated from the workers in the crowd.

Crutchfield gaveled the room quiet again.

"As to the housing conditions, the

mediation committee recommends that the United States Congress appoint a panel to investigate allegations of poor housing and unhealthy living conditions."

This time the farmers groaned out loud.

"Regarding allegations of police brutality and questionable conduct by other legal authorities, the committee recommends that the Governor of the State of California appoint a special panel to review police practices statewide and consider the publication of guidelines on police procedures."

Both sides roared at this one. The farmers and police expressed disdain at the decision, and the workers accused the committee of shirking the problem. One worker stood and shouted.

"Maybe you should give the police department a medal for pushing us around," he yelled.

At that point a scuffle ensued between his supporters and a couple of farmers who had been standing nearby. The police stepped in immediately to quell the situation. The man was taken from the room and Crutchfield gaveled the crowd into quiet.

"As to the question of wages, the mediation committee recommends the payment of 75 cents for every hundred pounds of cotton picked during this year's harvest."

The recommendation brought another roar from the audience. Neither side got what it wanted. The farmers had offered 60 cents, and the union had demanded $1. Many people felt the mediation had been a failure. The compromise wage satisfied nobody, and the mediation committee seemed to be dodging the other issues by recommending they be addressed by future committees. The problem was that few people believed these other committees would ever materialize.

Crutchfield gaveled the meeting to an end, and the committee members packed up their papers. The crowd began to disassemble, and Jake hung around for about a half-hour interviewing people who had been at the meeting.

"The whole meeting is a joke," said one worker.

"A waste of time," said a farmer.

"The only thing I can say is that I hope we can get past this now," a local merchant said. "We can't have people dying in the streets over a bunch of cotton."

The wage recommendation was not binding, but the only alternative was to keep fighting. Neither the farm owners nor the workers could afford to keep this up. The season was getting late, and one good rain could wipe out the entire cotton harvest. In that case, everyone would come out a loser. The 75-cent compromise was enough to get the harvest back in motion.

Nobody was completely happy, but the strike was over.

Chapter Twelve

The end of the strike seemed anti-climatic after all the hoopla. The jails had filled. The courts were clogged. And a total of eight farmers awaited trial accused of murder. But workers slipped back into the fields without fanfare. There were no celebrations.

The farmers had recruited workers from as far away as Texas, and even the strikers who returned to work faced a shortened harvest, because while they struck for better wages and conditions, destitute workers from other parts of the country worked for whatever wages they could get to survive.

By the time the strike was over about half of the cotton was already picked. So the union workers who had remained loyal to the strike found that non-union workers had picked much of the cotton at poverty wages.

To make matters worse, all the workers, both union and non-union, would remain destitute and move onto the next harvest in the Southern California and Arizona deserts to face the same problems they had hoped to solve in the San Joaquin Valley. In essence, it would start all over again.

Another complicating factor was the introduction of race into the situation. Ten to fifteen percent of the workers had been white from the very beginning. But these workers had always been part of the migrant farm worker population and had long ago reconciled themselves to the fact that they were in the same boat as their Mexican counterparts.

And in the process both groups had been desensitized to their cultural differences. In fact, the white farm workers even acquired some of the mannerisms of the Mexican workers. In some cases, the white workers actually spoke some Spanish.

But as a result of the dramatic influx of the so-called Okies into the agriculture fields of California -- partly due to the natural consequence of the Dust Bowl phenomenon, and partly due to the recruitment activities of the Farmers Association -- the racial make-up of the workers changed substantially. As the balance swung toward a white majority, racial tension among the workers increased.

These new arrivals were not interested in acquiring Mexican cultural mannerisms. They had a very different view of Mexicans, the same they held of blacks. They refused to work, let alone live, side by side with "dirty Mexicans."

Jake sat in his apartment one evening reading the newspapers that reported on other events throughout California. The strike had been over about a week, and it was nothing but a memory. Life returned to normal. The town bustled with activity.

The animosity between the workers and farmers had been set aside in order to complete the harvest. Next year was another story, and both hoped the economy would improve so they wouldn't have to go through this again.

As Jake sat in his shabby little room, there was a knock. He went to the door to find a trembling Veronica standing on the landing at the top of the stairs.

"What's the matter?" he asked. "You look white as a ghost."

"Some men are after me," she said.

"Come inside."

Jake stepped out onto the second floor landing and peered into the darkness until he was satisfied that they were alone. He thought he heard footsteps running away but couldn't see anyone.

He stepped back inside.

"Who are they?" He asked.

"I don't know. I was leaving Julianna's house and was waiting on the sidewalk in front for my ride. You probably don't know her. She was hospitalized for sun stroke and dehydration during the strike. I stayed at her place for a few days to help her get back on her feet.

"I was standing on the curb..."

Jake could see that she was rambling a little, apparently still shaken from the experience.

"...when they drove by me in a truck and said bad things. They insulted me and said how much they wanted me and what they would like to do to me. I ran away and ducked behind a building on the corner. It was a good thing I remembered where you lived. You were the closest person I knew of. I could not hope to find help anywhere else."

"I'm sorry Veronica. You're safe now. You can stay as long as you like."

"Maybe if I can have a drink of water and just sit for a minute. I will be leaving soon."

Jake and Veronica sat at what served as his kitchen table. Although it was the only table in the apartment, except for a small table next to his bed. He apologized for the lack of furniture.

"I have never had much money," he

said. "I don't have much to show for my life."

"I come from a modest family," she said. "We were never poor, not like many other people. We were luckier than most. But we never had a lot either."

"I have been wondering how it is you speak English so well," Jake said. "Have you been in this country long?"

"A few years. I came mostly for the work. I am like the rest of the workers in town. I move from harvest to harvest."

"What did you do in Mexico?" Jake asked

"My mother and father worked for the American Embassy in Mexico City for many years. She was a cook and housekeeper. And my father was a maintenance man. We lived in our own quarters over the garages in back.

"Most of the local employees lived outside the embassy grounds and came and went during normal working hours, except for special events. But the Ambassador's mother-in-law was a partial invalid.

"What I mean is that she could get around, but she needed a lot of help to take care of herself. She required on-call, live in care. My mother was well liked and offered to help. In return, the patron allowed us to live on the grounds.

"Our employers were very generous. They brought in tutors to teach their children, and they let me attend too. I grew up with English speaking children and learned my school lessons from English speaking tutors.

"I did quite well and had hopes of going to the university some day. The University of Mexico City sometimes lets poor children in when they show promise. But I guess it will never be."

"Why not?" he asked.

"When I became of age, I had to leave my parents' home. The Embassy budget did not provide for the care of adult children of their employees. And work was scarce. The Revolution destroyed our country; there were no jobs to be found. I decided to travel north in order to save enough to return and go to the university. But I don't make enough as a migrant worker to save any money."

"But maybe you will get to go back some day," Jake said.

"I think it is too late. I am too old now to get into the university; both of my parents are dead, and my family is broken. I had two older brothers who died fighting for Zapata, and my other two brothers moved north across the border. When I came, it was my desire to find them. But I haven't so far."

"Let's go sit on the sofa," Jake said. "It is more comfortable there."

"The only reason I stay with the union," she continued, "is because I hope some day I will reunite with what's left of my family. As long as I keep moving around, there is a chance I will find my brothers.

"I guess there is another reason: the union has been good to me. My ability to speak two languages has been a big help. As a woman, I probably will never be a union leader, but my supporting role is very rewarding. I feel I am making an important contribution. And because I grew up with American kids, I have adapted to life here very well. So if I never go back, that will be okay."

They continued their talk, and Jake learned a lot about Veronica. The topic turned to him.

"What about you?" she asked. "How do you come to be here?"

Jake told her of his background. He described the love affair between a white woman and Mexican man and how he felt that white society doomed his parents' relationship from the beginning.

"My mother was a woman ahead of her time," he said. "She was raised that it was the content of a person's inner self that mattered, not the color of their skin.

"My father was a good man, but he could not hold up under the pressure of the ostracism. My parents could not move to the white part of town; nobody would rent to them. My father's family said it was okay if they stayed at their house.

"My mother said that we lived behind my grandma's house for a couple of years, but my father was a proud man and he felt it was his obligation to move us to our own place as soon as we could afford it. Our lives were very poor, but my father would not move us back under his mother's roof, as he put it.

"The only work he could find was in agriculture, but when he hurt himself and could not work, he turned to alcohol. That was the beginning of the end between my mother and father. They split.

"From then on, it was only me and my mother until she died of tuberculosis.

He continued with the story of his childhood, the way in which he ended up at the newspaper, and the reason his name was changed from Juan to Jake. As he told her the story, he slowly became a little ashamed of himself. Veronica listened intently without showing any signs of judging him. But he knew that it sounded like he had been hiding behind his light colored skin rather than standing up and be proud of who he was.

He had convinced himself for years that he continued the lie because of his mother. But recently he began to question his courage. Was his mother really the reason why he did not face the truth? Or, was it that he simply did not have the cojones to face who he really was?

Veronica listened intently to his story.

"I guess that explains why you seemed so comfortable at the cantina," she said. "I would have guessed before we went there that you would have felt better on the other side of town. I was surprised that you took me there. But as it turns out, my people are your people too."

"Yes," he admitted. "I feel very much at home there. Actually, I am more at ease in the Mexican side of town than on the white side of town. I have seen white culture through a very unique set of eyes. They have spoken to me in ways they never would if they knew who I really am. White people are too full of themselves."

As they continued their conversation, Jake felt an overwhelming urge to kiss Veronica. As she talked, he looked at her face, her neckline, her hair. He watched her lips move as she spoke. He visually traced the line of her chin, the form of her eyebrows, the curve of her ears. He heard less and less of what she was saying as time went on. He was lost in her beauty.

After a while, both seemed talked out. They had learned quite a bit about each other. Finally, after a couple of minutes of silence, Veronica announced that it was time to go.

"I am sure the men are gone by now," she said as she stood up. "Maybe it is best if I leave before it gets too late."

Jake stood up and took her by the hand.

"Don't go," he said.

She looked directly into his eyes.

"What are you thinking," she asked.

"This is what I am thinking," he said as he leaned down to kiss her.

She responded to his kiss without hesitation. The two embraced passionately for a couple of minutes as they kissed. Suddenly, she pulled away.

"Can anybody see us from the street," she asked.

He stepped toward the door and flipped off the light switch.

"Probably not, but that should take care of it."

They returned to their embrace, this time with less inhibition.

Both of them began to breathe heavily. She was much smaller than him and had to stretch to meet his lips. She wrapped her arms around his neck. As their passion increased, Jake reached for her breasts. Veronica welcomed the overture, and Jake went further by slipping his hands up her blouse. He palmed both of her generous breasts for a brief few seconds, when Veronica slowly pulled away.

Thinking the encounter was ended, Jake could only smile as instead Veronica unbuttoned her blouse. Having removed her top, she helped Jake unbutton his shirt. They returned to their previous embrace, both now bare to the waist.

Feeling each other's nakedness sparked a new level of passion, and the two lovers fumbled with each other's remaining clothing, sneaking in a kiss and caress as the clothes continued to come off.

Now they were standing completely naked in the middle of the room, kissing and fondling each other as any two young people might who were physically experiencing each other for the first time.

Jake stopped briefly and took her by the hand, leading her to the bed where they would make passionate love until exhausted. The two laid on the bed in a close embrace, bathed in sweat from the encounter and the warm night air.

They laid next to each other as the moonlight peered into the room, illuminating their nakedness.

"You have a beautiful body," Jake said.

"Thank you," she responded, trying to hide her obvious embarrassment.

She did not cover herself, however. She might have been a little embarrassed, but she was not ashamed. Jake's remark was not empty flattery either. She was a beautiful woman, and as Jake continued to appreciate the look of her body, feelings for her re-emerged. He wanted her again, and she matched his desire with her own.

Somewhere during the night the two fell asleep. Veronica awakened to discover that dawn was peeking into the room. Suddenly, she bolted upright and Jake woke up to the movement.

"It's morning," she said. "I must leave."

"Why?" Jake asked. "Let me buy us some breakfast."

"I must not be seen leaving your apartment with you, and certainly not at this hour. It wouldn't be right. People would talk."

"I don't care what people think," Jake said.

"I do," she said as she quickly dressed.

"When will I see you again?" Jake asked.

"Soon," she said. "I will come by your office."

Veronica moved toward the door, and they kissed. She asked that he look to see if anyone was around who might see her leave, but the door to his upstairs apartment was on the back of the building. So there was little chance anyone was around.

Veronica slipped out quickly and quietly, and Jake was left alone with his thoughts. He knew that he must have her. He had never been much of a ladies man, although he had his share, he supposed. But this was different. He had never felt about a woman like he did about Veronica. He would do everything he could to keep her.

The next few days went by with agonizing slowness. Jake hoped to see Veronica, and every moment of his imagination was filled with her image. He could not shake the thought of her to the point that his work even suffered. Unfortunately, the news did not stop, and Jake had a job to do.

He did not have an inventory of merchandise that sold itself like a mercantile store. He had to create his product, and he had to do it on a regular basis. There was no respite.

Jake continued to publish articles about the legacy of the strike. The refugee camp, for instance, had been abandoned. And the trash left behind turned out to be a headache for the property owner. Jake had never found out who owned the property, although it would have been easy enough to do by simply going down to the County Recorder's Office.

But he decided to do the owner a favor. Letting the world in on his secret could have resulted in some serious consequences. The property owner had sided with the enemy by lending his land to the union, and the Farmers Association would never forgive or forget.

Jake had learned, however, that in return for the use of the land the union workers had picked the owner's crop for free. But that bit of information was probably irrelevant now.

The court system purged itself of its clogged agenda. Pat Chambers had been convicted of Criminal Syndicalism and sent to prison for five years, as were several of his union cohorts.

Jake would learn several years later that other laws like the one that allowed the courts to jail Chambers as a so-called subversive would also allow the federal government to place Japanese citizens in concentration camps just a few miles away from the San Joaquin Valley, just because they were Japanese. The times were not very forgiving to those who did not fit into a narrow definition of a patriot.

The ultimate fate of the CAWIU also became news. Jake read in the San Jose Mercury that the union headquarters had been raided by a farmers' group of special police; a printing press was destroyed, along with a room full of records. Two union officials had been hospitalized. The life of the CAWIU was nearly at an end after that raid.

Solomon Wirinski left for Southern California, where he expected to spend the next several weeks recovering, and the eight farmers accused of the Citrus Grove killings would go to trial the first of December.

It was the end of October, and the harvest was nearly at an end. Jake was amazed at how much had occurred in such a short period. The strike had lasted five weeks, and the harvest was nearly in, just in time for the fall rainy season.

Jake and Sally worked on some classified ads when the door bell sounded, and Jake looked up to see Veronica. His day was made.

"Hi," he said. "How are you?"

"Fine," she said.

"Can I buy you some coffee?"

Sally jerked her head up when he said that.

"Sure."

The couple walked down the street toward the diner.

"I have to tell you that I am leaving," she said suddenly.

"Leaving," he said.

"Where are you going?"

"Julianna is feeling better, and the picking will be done in a couple of days. I will be leaving after that."

Jake stopped on the sidewalk in the middle of the block and turned to her.

"Where will you go?"

"I am going to go to the Imperial Valley.

Tomatoes will be ready for picking the first of the year. I must be there early if I am to get hired on with a good grower."

"But what about us?" He asked.

"I love you," Jake. "I think I have known this from the very first. I admired the way you stood up for a boy you didn't even know. But I have thought a lot in the last couple of days, and we have no future together."

"What do you mean no future?"

"How would I make a living here? How would you make a living if you are seen spending time with me in public? White people would not approve of their newspaper owner being involved with a Mexican."

"But...

"Let me finish before I come apart. I have thought a lot about this. I would hope we could have a future together, Jake, but you aren't even comfortable with who you are. You hide from the world. You don't want anyone to know that you are Mexican. I understand why you do this, but I must be with a man who is proud of who he is. I do not want live a lie. I don't know whether to call you Jake or Juan."

Jake was hurt, but he realized that she was right. He must find himself before he could make anyone else happy.

271

"I understand," he said with his eyes welling up. "Will I see you before you go?"

Veronica could not contain herself.

"No," she said nearly bursting into tears. "I would change my mind and stay, and I would just be in the way."

"I can't talk you out of this, can I?" he asked with a knowing look on his face.

"No," she said. "But I will never forget you."

"Will you be back next season?" Jake asked.

"Probably," she said. "I have to harvest. I have no other choices."

The two of them embraced on the sidewalk. They lingered in that position, neither one wanting to let go.

"I'd better go," she said. "People are watching."

Jake let her go, and they exchanged a last loving glance.

"Goodbye," she said as she walked away.

Why was he letting her go? But what could he do? She had thought the situation through and was doing what she thought was the best for him. Marriage had not been discussed, so she had not been offered a secure relationship, and she was right when she said that he had some things to work out.

He watched her walk down the street until he became conscious of some people watching him. He turned and walked back to his office. He had a horrible emptiness in his chest.

Call Me Juan

Chapter Thirteen

Jake could not get back to work. He carried his hurt around everywhere. It was only the coming of the murder trial that finally brought him out of his distraction. The trial began in early December, and it was expected to be the biggest news event to hit the town since its conception, second only, perhaps, to the killings themselves. Other murders had occurred in this area, but the accused had not been prominent members of the community.

Eight defendants were charged with various crimes, including murder, manslaughter, assault with a deadly weapon, and illegal weapon possession, although the charges would change before the trial began. Each defendant had his own lawyer, even though they would be tried together. The charges were for crimes against the same victims.

Extra tables had to be brought into the courtroom to accommodate eight defendants and their lawyers. The gallery was full everyday, but the first phase of the trial concentrated on jury selection. Even the balcony was full, and the carnival-like atmosphere seemed to suggest the proceedings were not being taken seriously.

The defendants enjoyed themselves as they arrived each day to an outward show of support from their family and friends. Audience members extended their hands and patted the defendants on the back as they passed. Finding an objective jury should have been of great concern, but the judge easily sat 12 jurors the first day, which Jake commented about in his first editorial about the trial.

"It took less than an hour for Judge Frank Overton to appoint 12 local residents to the Citrus Grove murder jury," the editorial read. "The jury was made up of all white men, and several members had clear ties to the farming industry."

"Only two people were challenged by the prosecution as being unfavorable, one was an old man who could not hear well, and the other was a young man of 18 years old, who obviously was not taking the process seriously. If the judge had wanted to pre-determine the outcome of the trial," Jake continued, "he could not have chosen a better group of people to serve on this jury."

Jake's comments solicited outrage by the Farmers Association, and advertising to the newspaper dropped by half before the trial got underway. Jake's next edition would be much smaller, since he needed the revenue from advertising to pay his printing bills. He was determined to press on.

The trial started with a bang. The County District Attorney, George Green, called his first witness, a truck driver who had been in town the day of the killings.

"Do you swear to tell the truth, the whole truth, and nothing but the truth?" asked the bailiff.

"I do."

"State your name."

"John Colton."

District Attorney Green proceeded with his case.

"Mr. Colton, what is your occupation?"

"I drive a truck."

"Is it true that you were in Citrus Grove on Tuesday, October 10?"

"Yes, I was."

"What was it that caused you to be in Citrus Grove on that day?"

"I work for Amalgamated Fertilizer in Gunderson, and I make regular stops in several towns in the county. Citrus Grove is on my regular route."

"Did you see anything unusual on the day in question?"

"Yes. There was a large group of people lingering in front of the Union Hall. I was coming out of the pharmacy, when a bunch of cars and trucks pulled up in front of the Hall. Quite a few men armed with guns got out of the cars and began yelling at the people in the street."

"What happened then?"

"The armed men charged into the crowd, swinging their guns, and a few of the men shot into the building. When the guns went off, the crowd panicked and fist-fights broke out."

"Were you in a position to see the fate of those who were killed?"

"Only one," Colton said.

"Explain what you saw."

"I saw that man...," he said pointing to the table of defendants as the district attorney interrupted.

"Be specific, which man?"

"The tall man with the graying hair sitting second from the right."

"Let the record show that Mr. Colton has identified George Applebee."

"So noted," said the judge. "Continue."

"I saw George Applebee," Colton said, "shoot a man in the side of the head and then fire a second shot as the man reeled to the side and then fall backwards."

"Could you describe the victim?"

"He was probably in his thirties, dark skinned, not too tall with black hair."

"Please note that Mr. Colton has described Rogelio Roblero."

"We have a picture of the shooting victim. Is this the man you saw?"

"Yes," Colton said.

The audience began to talk excitedly among themselves.

"Let the record show that Mr. Colton has identified a picture of Roblero as the man who was killed in the riot. Please note that the District Attorney's Office has submitted a copy of the Coroner's report on the death of Rogelio Roblero. He was shot twice through the side of the head by a .22 Caliber pistol.

"The District Attorney's Office also submits the gun that killed Mr. Roblero. It is registered to the defendant, George Applebee.

The audience reacted again to the testimony, this time loud enough for the judge to gavel them into silence.

"Did Mr. Roblero have anything in his hands that you could see?"

"No," Colton said.

"I have nothing else for this witness, your honor," the district attorney said. "Your witness."

The defendant's lawyer, Ryan Rhondel, had a reputation for being at the top of his profession. He immediately went to work trying to muddle Colton's damning testimony.

"According to the police report, other witnesses stated that Mr. Roblero had a club in his hand. How do you explain why you didn't see it?"

"By other witnesses do you mean friends of the defendant?" Colton asked with a broad smile on his face.

The audience broke into a roaring laugh, and the judge couldn't hear Rhondel's objection.

Judge Overton gaveled the gallery into silence.

"I object to this man's response and ask that it be stricken from the record," Rhondel said.

"The objection is sustained. The jury will disregard Mr. Colton's last statement."

"How can you be so sure that Mr. Roblero did not have a weapon in his hand?" Rhondel asked.

"I had a clear view of the man who was

shot, and I was only about 20 feet away. There is no doubt that the victim was empty handed. He never saw what hit him."

"Objection!" Rhondel yelled.

"Sustained."

"I have no further questions of this witness your honor."

"You are dismissed," said Judge Overton.

Colton stepped down from the witness box.

"I would like to call Robert Jefferson as my next witness," said the prosecution.

"State your name for the record please," the bailiff said.

"Robert Jefferson."

"Mr. Jefferson, please state your occupation."

"I am the owner and operator of Bob's Barbershop."

"Would you please tell us the location of your business?"

"It is located at 331 Main Street, next door to The Citrus Grove Pharmacy, directly across the street from the Union Hall."

"Mr. Jefferson, can you tell me where you were at 11:35 a.m. on the day in question?"

"I was standing outside of my store on

the sidewalk."

"What were you doing on the sidewalk? Wouldn't you usually be inside attending to your business?

"Yes, but I was outside watching the activities. There were hundreds of people standing in the street, waiting for the union rally to begin. I went out to see what was going on."

"Were you outside when the shooting for which these defendants are accuse took place?"

"Yes, I was."

"Please tell this court in as much detail as possible what you witnessed."

"I was standing outside my shop," Jefferson said, "as the street began to fill with people. As I watched, several cars full of men arrived in the midst of the crowd.

"I watched while the men got out of their cars, some were already armed, and some got weapons from the trunks of their cars. The armed men began shouting things like 'communists go home' and 'you Mexicans go back where you belong.'"

"What happened next?" D.A. Green asked.

"All of a sudden the armed men broke

into a run and charged the crowd. The crowd seemed to explode. Shots were fired; fist fights broke out, and the armed men went into a frenzy. I saw a woman being attacked while another woman came to her aid. The first woman was being pistol whipped by that man."

"Please be specific Mr. Jefferson," prosecutor Green said. "Exactly which man?"

"He is the man over there, sitting on the far right of the defendant's table."

"Let the record reflect that the witness has identified William Stern."

"So noted," said the judge.

"What happened next?"

"I ran to help the poor woman, but it was too late. The man had already shot her, and she fell to the ground. The man who shot her then stood over her and shot her again while she was lying in the street on her back."

"Let the record show that the woman named Juanita Nunez died on her way to the hospital of massive bleeding from the two gunshot wounds."

"Go on," said the district attorney.

"I grabbed the arm of the other woman and pulled her to safety. The man who shot the woman who lay on the ground turned his gun on us but did not fire. He looked at me and turned away.

"Are you absolutely sure about the facts of the shooting you witnessed?"

"Yes, it happened right in front of me. I was lucky to get away with my life."

"Objection," said Rhondel.

Rhondel had by now taken charge of the defense of all the accused. Although the other lawyers were present, they clearly had deferred to Rhondel's reputation.

"Sustained," the judge said.

Testimony went on for two days. Each witness verified in one way or another the circumstances of the incident. The county coroner verified the causes of death. Witness after witness agreed that the victims had been unarmed.

Jake's friend Gordy was the prosecution's last witness.

"Will Gordon Wilcock please take the stand?"

The bailiff swore him in.

"Deputy Wilcock, we have had exhaustive testimony about the facts of this case from eyewitness, so I will restrict my questions to you about the circumstances that have been revealed as a result of your police investigation. Do you understand?"

"Yes, I do."

"The police report says that when being questioned several of the accused stated that they were shot upon first. Did the police investigation shed any light on the contention that union members fired upon any of the accused?" Green asked.

"Several members of the department searched the walls of buildings up and down Main Street for a block in each direction. We found 26 bullet holes on the front of the Union Hall building, but we found no bullet holes anywhere else."

"If the accused had been correct about being fired upon, what investigative methods would be used in your investigation that might corroborate their stories?"

"We thoroughly inspected the cars that had transported the accused, and we searched the walls of all of the buildings across the street from the Union Hall."

"Why would you search the walls of those buildings?" the prosecutor asked.

"The accused had parked their cars on the street opposite from the Union Hall building. The accused were between the crowd in front of the Union Hall and the buildings across the street. If shots had been fired in their direction from the Union Hall building, bullet holes would have been found either in the sides of the cars that were facing the crowd or in the walls of the buildings behind the accused. Those walls would have acted as backstops."

"Did you find any bullet holes anywhere?"

"No, we did not"

The audience responded with quite a bit of discussion. The judge banged his gavel.

"Please be quiet in the gallery," he said.

"Does your investigation shed light in any other way about the contention that the accused were fired upon at any time before or during, the melee?"

"Yes, we were unable to find anyone other than the defendants who saw weapons in the possession of the victims or any other person connected with the rally. We also interviewed every shop owner on both sides of the street within reasonable sight of the Union Hall building and everyone who said they saw what happened, and nobody stated that they had seen any weapons in the hands of anyone other than the accused."

The gallery broke into an uproar this time, and it took longer for the judge to quiet the audience.

"I cannot tolerate this kind of outburst. If the people in the gallery cannot contain themselves, I will clear the courtroom," the judge said.

"What can you tell me about the capture of the defendants?" the District Attorney asked.

"Several deputies arrived," Wilcock said, "assessed the situation and went in pursuit of the fleeing perpetrators. Three miles away, the deputies who pursued the cars that had been described by witnesses ran into a group of vehicles that were being detained for speeding by members of the California Highway Patrol.

"Once the deputies compared information with the state patrolmen, it was determined that the men who were being detained were the same who were accused of the incident in town."

"Were the defendants questioned at that time?"

"Yes, at first they denied any involvement. But after the cars were searched and the guns were found, they told us that they had been fired upon and were acting in self defense."

"In other words, they changed their

stories once the guns had been found?"

"Objection," Rhondel said.

"Overruled," the judge said.

"There has also been testimony that the sheriff's department did not have the manpower to deal with the overwhelming problems resulting throughout the county due to the strike. As a result, special deputies were sworn in to help. Were any of the defendants acting as special deputies for the department you represent?"

"No, they were not."

"Were they acting on behalf of any other law enforcement agency?"

"No."

"How can you know this for sure?"

"I spoke with all the law enforcement organizations in the County," Wilcock said.

"So, none of the defendants were acting in any official capacity, is that your testimony?"

"Yes, it is."

"Thank you deputy," Green said. "I have no further questions of this witness."

The deputy was questioned by two of the defendant's lawyers, but it was clear that they had little to ask. Gordy was a seasoned courtroom veteran and simply answered the questions that the prosecutor had asked without personal comment or the introduction of personal opinion. There was little that lawyers for the defense could do with his testimony.

The prosecution rested, and court was adjourned for the weekend.

Jake had been generally satisfied that the court proceedings were being conducted in a professional manner. There was no reason to believe at this point that the outcome would be anything but fair.

The prosecution's case seemed overwhelming. Monday Jake would be present to hear what the defense had to say.

The weekend passed quickly. Jake had managed to get another edition out during the trial, but his advertising was drying up, and the newspaper became smaller and smaller. He already had to let Sally go, and he was a week late on the office rent. He owned his equipment, but it was old and not worth very much. He had nothing of value that could be used as collateral for a loan. But even if he had, he doubted there was a bank anywhere that didn't have close ties to the farmers.

If things kept going like this, he figured his business would collapse within a couple of months. He probably would make it through the trial, but the community was going to have to come to his rescue after that. He hoped that after the trial was over, everything would settle down. His only other option was to change the tone of his reporting and revert back to being a farmer cheerleader.

But it may be too late even for that. No, he had made his choice: tell it the way he saw it and let the community decide the fate of his business. He had a glimmer of hope, however, because he began to have more and more people compliment him on his reporting. Maybe there was still a chance.

Monday morning arrived and the court was packed again. Jake determined that like Friday, the makeup of the gallery was an equal mixture of farm worker and farm owner. As he contemplated this dynamic, he daydreamed that his next headlined might read: *Courtroom Explodes into Riot.* He didn't expect this to happen. He knew most of the people present, and most of them were decent people of both colors, just curious. But a courtroom riot was fun to think about.

"At least I could go out in a blaze of glory," Jake thought to himself with a wry chuckle.

The bailiff stood up and shouted: "Will

the court please rise, Judge Overton presiding."

The defense was routine. There were no witnesses available who could dispute all of the evidence. The cause of death was clear. Eyewitness testimony directly identified those who were responsible for the deaths. The eyewitnesses were very credible. None of them had anything to gain by lying. The farmers had been caught red-handed. By now, everyone knew what had happened, how and who did it. The only testimony the defense could produce was in the form of character reference, which is exactly what happened.

Defense attorneys paraded one character witness after another. The accused were portrayed as decent family men with no arrest records. Jake found this interesting, however, since a couple of them did have arrest records for drunk and disorderly or domestic disputes. Jake had not reported the arrests for fear of retaliation. He wished that he would have. It was the public's right to know these things, particularly under these extraordinary circumstances.

The prosecutor did not challenge the contention by the defense attorney that the accused were perfect citizens. He certainly had access to the arrest reports. By not doing his job, Jake realized now that he had become part of this cover-up.

"Sol should be here to see this," Jake thought to himself.

Testimony ended with little accomplished for the three days that it took to complete the defense's case. The next phase was closing arguments.

Early the following morning the lead council for the defense presented his closing statement. He had no facts to support a not guilty verdict, but he was fully aware that he had the advantage. He was preaching to the choir.

"Gentlemen," he began, "Several months ago this county was invaded by thousands of criminals. Our jails filled; our courts could not deal with all of the crimes; and our police forces had to deputize private citizens to keep from being overwhelmed. Decent citizens could not walk down the street without fear for their personal safety."

Jake thought back to the first Sunday when he had to intervene on behalf of that young man.

"Who was the criminal that day?" he thought to himself.

"In our society we expect our last line

of defense to be the front doors of our homes; that is why our Constitution gives us the right to bear arms. When law enforcement cannot protect us any longer, our fathers and brothers become protectors of our women and our property. This is who we are as a people.

"Men have come among us, unhygienic, godless, communistic people whose only interest is in undermining our very existence. The men you see before you answered the call of defense of their homes.

"Law enforcement could not do it. Our government could not do it. Where were these men supposed to turn except to themselves and each other, which is their right under the Constitution?"

"Who among you would act differently if you believed your women and children were in danger? Who among you would stand by idly and watch their communities crumble in the face of such an invasion?

"I submit to the gentlemen on the jury that when called upon to save your property and your families each of you would respond in the same way. As a result, your duty here is to free these men. They were only doing what our society expected of them. Thank you."

The defense remarks caused quite a stir

among the gallery. The response was subdued because everyone believed the judge when he threatened to clear the gallery if its members got out of control again. But the judge normally would have gaveled the gallery into silence anyway in order to resume the case. However, he let the gallery talk for several minutes before rapping his gavel. To Jake it seemed clear that the judge wanted the defense's words to take full effect. There would have been no other reason for his hesitation. Jake had seen this ploy before. It was a tactic that allowed the jury extended time to think about the remarks.

When the prosecutor stepped forward, the judge pounded his gavel. It was the state's turn.

Jake had attended many court cases where District Attorney Green had been the lead prosecutor. He had a reputation for being flamboyant and passionate. He hated to lose, and he used every courtroom theatric he could get away with. Jake was expecting quite a show…but it didn't materialize.

Green made a simple statement. He briefly went over the evidence and said the men were guilty. The statement was dispassionate, even boring and lasted only a couple of minutes. It seemed clear to Jake that the prosecutor's career could be on the line. His presentation had been professional but not tough.

Now it was the turn of the judge. The only thing that remained was instructions to the jury.

Eight defendants faced charges of first degree murder, second degree murder, inciting a riot and criminal conspiracy. There were a total of 32 counts that the jury was expected to contemplate, four charges per man.

"I want to address the jury before you confer on the charges," the judge said. "What is important to understand here is that we have eight defendants. All are being charged for the same crimes. It would be inappropriate for you to find them guilty or innocent individually. Either they are all guilty, or they are not.

"The defendants cite self-defense as justification for their actions," the judge continued. "If you determine that these men in fact did commit the actions they are charged with, your next responsibility is to decide if self defense justifies their actions. In that case, your decision must be not guilty. I commit you to your duties."

The bailiff escorted the jury to the jury room, and the judge retired to his private chambers. The gallery was left to its own thoughts and comments.

Jake left with a sinking feeling. The all-or-nothing jury instructions seemed to pre-ordain the outcome. No jury in this valley would convict all eight defendants for the murder of two people simply because they were present on the same street at the same time as those who actually pulled the trigger.

Jake was now convinced that the trial was just a show, that the outcome was clear. Still, it would probably be days for the jury to kick around 32 individual charges. There was nothing to do but wait.

Jake was stunned when two hours later the announcement was in that the jury had reached a conclusion. The court was called back together the following morning to hear the outcome. The gallery assembled to hear the judge ask for the jury's ruling.

"Mr. Foreman, have you reached a verdict? The judge asked.

"Yes, your honor. We find the defendants not guilty on all charges by reason of self-defense."

Jake couldn't believe his ears. The jury had decided 32 criminal charges in less than two hours, including lunch.

"All of this for nothing," he said out loud to himself. "Sol was right. The workers never had a chance."

Call Me Juan

Chapter Fourteen

Jake Rogers awoke to the hum of his house fan. He did not know what time it was, but from the angle of the sun beating down through the window to the foot of his bed, he guessed it was about noon.

San Joaquin Valley weather could be pleasant in January. The rain could be nice; it cleaned up the air. The primary problem with the rain was the fog that usually came later. Jake didn't like the fog. It was depressing. He remembered reading some place that the highest suicide rate in the country was in Seattle.

"I'll bet they have a lot of fog up there," he thought to himself.

But today was going to be sunny, good for one's disposition.

Jake put the coffee on and shuffled to the window in his underwear. He leaned out the window and looked up and down the dirt street, finding it hard to believe that just a few months ago two people had been brutally murdered there. Now it was as if nothing had happened. A stray dog lay on the wooden boardwalk across the street. A couple of cars were parked in front of the bank. Otherwise Citrus Grove appeared to be a ghost town.

Jake drank coffee while he dressed.

He couldn't seem to get started today. He

finally decided to go downstairs to his office, where he spent the next hour or so looking over area newspapers and trying to generate a plan for his next issue.

The bell rang to the office front door. Jake looked up to see Sally standing at the counter.

"Hey kid," Jake said. "How are you doing?"

"Just fine, Jake. I was in the area and thought I would drop in and say hello."

"Great! So what's new with you these days?"

"Not much. I have been looking for work, but there is not much here in town. The Globe offered me a job, but I can't get there. It is too far."

"Things are tough everywhere. You might consider taking the job. There is always some way to get around. You need to be creative. These days people are doing things that under normal circumstances they wouldn't do. Have you talked to their   shipping   department? The Globe has regular newspaper drop off sites all over the county, including Citrus Grove. Maybe you can hitch a ride."

"That's not a bad idea, but I was hoping you could take me back," she said.

"I would love to, Sally, but I can barely make ends meet. If things don't get better soon, I may have to close down all together."

"Sorry to hear that, Jake. I guess there is a

price to pay for sticking your neck out. Was it worth it?"

"I guess only time will tell."

"Well, just thought I would say hello. I think I will follow your suggestion and give the Globe shipping department a call. Talk to you later."

"Goodbye, Sally. And good luck?"

The front door bell rang again as she left.

Jake lost interest in what he was doing and decided to get a bite to eat. His stomach was growling, and he realized that he hadn't eaten all day.

Barney's was dead. It was the middle of the afternoon. The lunch crowd was gone, and dinner hadn't started yet, and if Barney started drinking, dinner was probably out of the question.

Jake ordered a sandwich and grabbed a newspaper that was sitting on the edge of the table next to him.

He browsed through the pages, trying to get some ideas. He noticed a small item on an inside page that the tomato harvest was about to begin in the Imperial Valley. He felt a twinge in his chest. Veronica would be there looking for work.

Jake went on to other news. President Roosevelt announced a U.S. oil embargo against Japan.

"Oh great," Jake thought out loud. "I wonder what will come of that."

He finished his lunch and decided to take a

drive in Barney's car. The sun was nice, although it was a little cool. But it was a pleasant afternoon.

Without thinking about it, Jake found himself at the old site of the Corcoran camp. He got out and reminisced about the strike. As horrible as it was at times, it was exciting. Jake had never experienced anything like it before. It was almost like he missed it, while at the same time he hoped never to see anything like it again.

He walked through the camp remembering how it was organized.

"The water tank was over there," he thought to himself. "And it was over there where the main tent was located."

He also remembered how that first time Veronica had showed him around. He guessed that he was already in love with her by then but hadn't known it yet.

"I wonder what she is doing right at this moment," he thought. "I wonder if I will ever see her again."

Now in a state of depression, he decided to go to La Cantina del Sol for a beer. Jake didn't like to drink during the day, but it would be about five o'clock by the time he got there. A cold beer sounded pretty good right now.

At the cantina Jake was lost in his thoughts. He found a seat near the back door and sat quietly, drinking several beers before he decided to go home.

Once he got up, he realized that he had drunk more than he had intended. He left Barney's car at the cantina and decided to walk home. It wasn't really very far, and he wasn't in any hurry, so it took a little more time than it normally would.

Jake arrived at his place and slowly ascended the steps at the back of the building. His apartment looked even more dreary than normal. He laid on his bed without taking the time to undress and stared at the ceiling for a few minutes before falling asleep.

He wasn't sure what time it was, but he awoke coughing uncontrollably. In his stupor he was unable to compute the circumstances surrounding him at that moment. It took a few seconds to fully appreciate what was happening. His apartment was on fire!

He bolted upright and looked around to see the room full of smoke, but he didn't see any flames, at least not at first.

His first thought was to get out of the building and raise an alarm. He went to the back door and couldn't get it open. The door was jammed.

"Damn it," he said out loud.

He forced his body against the door in an attempt to loosen it, but the door wouldn't budge. Next he leaned back a little and crashed his body into the door. It finally gave, but when he opened the door he discovered that the stairs were engulfed in flames.

Realizing he was trapped, he grabbed a chair and threw it into the front window. He might have simply opened it, but between the residual alcohol in his system and his half asleep state he wasn't thinking very well. A little panic preempted his otherwise normally good judgment.

He climbed out on the overhang that sheltered the boardwalk underneath, crawled to the edge and dropped to the dirt street below.

He heard in the background someone yell fire. He heard another voice, then several, and the town came alive in what seemed like seconds.

He stood motionless for a few minutes while residents arrived with buckets of water. The volunteer fire department was close behind.

From what he could tell, the fire apparently started in his office on the ground floor. The fire department fought the fire for about an hour before it was brought under control. As Jake stood there and watched his house and livelihood both evaporate before his eyes at the same time, Delgado appeared at this side.

"Que lastima," his friend said. "What will you do now?"

"That's a good question. I guess my first step is to find some place to spend the night."

"You need not worry about that. You will stay with us."

"Muchas gracias, mi amigo," Jake said. "Vamos a la casa."

Jake returned to his shop the following morning after a few hours sleep. He walked around the building to assess the damage. It looked like someone had thrown a bucket full of gas into the window downstairs. He apparently also splashed gas on the back of the building before igniting it. That would account for the fact that his stairs were on fire when Jake had tried to get out.

Jake walked around to the front of the building and entered through the main door. The fire had apparently spread quickly. The building was old and the wood was dry. It wouldn't take much to get a good fire going.

He looked at his equipment, desk and chair, paste up tables, files.

"Total loss," he said to himself in a low tone.

He went back outside and walked into the middle of the street to get a look at the overall picture. Much of the outside structure was still intact. The owner could rebuild if he wanted to.

"Tough break Jake," said a voice behind him. "I guess your luck ran out after all."

Jake turned to see John J. standing in the middle of the street with a grin on his face.

"Luck had nothing to do with this J.J.," Jake commented. "This was arson, and the man who did this better hope he doesn't get caught. This is a prison offense. The owner of this property was a land owner who doesn't like your father."

"What does my father have to do with this?"

"Well," Jake said, "this looks like the work of a barn burner, you know, like the barn you burned down a few years ago. In that case, your father was able to buy you out of it. In this case, the building owner is not afraid of your dad and probably will press charges."

"Better watch what you say, Jake. You could get hurt for talking like that."

"Never mind," Jake said. "I am sure something will be worked out. It always is."

"What ever happened to that lawyer friend of yours?" J.J. asked, recovering from Jake's remarks and going back on the offensive.

Jake realized that he was being baited and decided this could be the showdown that he had been expecting some day. But he had to play his cards right. John J. was a big man. Jake needed to be careful here.

"He is okay. I got a letter from him last week. He is in the Imperial Valley. It seems there an agriculture union down there that is threatening a strike." Jake said as he moved a little closer.

"I guess they never learn, do they Jake?"

"Perhaps not."

"That is what I have always liked about you," J.J.

said. "You talk good. Did you learn to talk like that because you run a newspaper?"

"No, it is because I went to school, J.J. Unlike you, I made it past the third grade."

Jake could see that J.J. was getting mad. He needed for this to happen. Jake new that fighting J.J. would be like a matador fighting a bull, finesse versus shear strength. Jake had to out think J.J.; Jake knew he couldn't go against J.J. without an edge. Getting J.J. mad would make him lose control. In that case, his size wouldn't be as much of an advantage.

"You think you are smart, don't you Jake?"

"Not so smart, J.J. If I was smart, you would be in jail instead of out on the street acting like an idiot."

J.J. turned red. It was as if he was a tea kettle about to explode. Jake moved even closer.

Jake continued to push J.J. over the edge.

"In fact, I suspect that you are so stupid that the only reason that your father keeps you out of jail is to have someone to burn buildings down and beat up boys."

J.J. pulled his arm back to wind up for a big punch and Jake was ready for it. Jake let out a lightening straight left to J.J.'s nose. The swiftness of Jake's punch caught J.J. before he could follow though with his own punch.

Jake had been sizing up his first punch as J.J. talked. He knew from experience that the nose was a sensitive spot, and that it didn't take much to break it. One only had to hit it at the right angle. Jake also knew that a broken nose would cause the eyes to tear, which would give Jake as many as several seconds advantage while J.J. collected himself, seconds that would be precious if Jake were to put the big man down.

Jake followed with three immediate and successive straight lefts as he tried to set up his opponent for a knockout punch. With blazing speed, Jake moved in as J.J. reeled backward. Jake continued with his left while he tried to set up his opponent for a big right. The timing had to be perfect, Jake reasoned. He might only have one chance.

Jake saw his opening, moved in with his left foot and put all of his weight into the punch. Jake connected with a right to the cheek that split the flesh to the bone and sent the big man to the dirt.

If it had been the other way around, Jake knew that J.J. would have put the boots to his downed opponent. But as much as J.J. might have deserved it, Jake couldn't bring himself to do it, a choice he would regret.

J.J. sat on his behind dazed from the blows. He tried to shake it off as some people began coming out of the stores to see what was happening. J.J.'s face was already a mass of blood. Even Jake was amazed at how a few well placed, calculated punches could do so much damage.

A broken nose could bleed quite a bit, giving the injured man the impression that he was worse off than he really was. That could give Jake a psychological edge if nothing else.

The problem was that J.J. was a very strong man, and Jake had given him too much chance to revive. J.J. stood up and beat a little of the dust off of his pants. He looked at Jake with a sinister smile on his face, and Jake knew he was in trouble.

J.J. rushed his opponent, but Jake was much more nimble and managed to sidestep J.J.'s attempt to tackle him. J.J. did manage, however, to get his arm around Jake's waist as he tried to sidestep the big man's maneuver. But in the process Jake was able to land a looping left to the side of J.J.'s head. J.J. was already off balance, so the punch sent the big man face first again into the dirt. Jake had partially used the bigger man's own weight against him, and J.J.'s momentum sent him into a second meeting with the street.

A crowd was now beginning to form, and Jake could hear a few shouts of encouragement. But he still couldn't bring himself to kick J.J. when he was down. Besides, Jake didn't just want to beat the man, he wanted to humiliate him. It was only J.J.'s reputation as a bully that gave him status in Citrus Grove. Without that, he would be nothing. If he was not feared, he would be reduced to the town clown.

"You look pretty silly down there on your ass," Jake said sarcastically. "Let me help you up."

Jake knew that his comment with further enrage his opponent, and he counted on that.

J.J. jumped to his feet and tried to grab Jake this time. J.J.'s size would be Jake's end if they got into a wrestling match. Jake knew his only chance was to stay on his feet and keep hitting J.J. from a distance.

Jake peppered J.J. with short rights and lefts in quick succession, and gave him another big right that was intended to drop the big man, but this time he didn't go down and managed instead to turn the tables on Jake. J.J. was more than a bully; he was a brawler who was used to taking punches. J.J. got a right hand in of his own that opened a cut on Jake's left cheek. Jake's head seemed to explode, and he saw stars for a couple of seconds.

By now the crowd was getting pretty large as people from all over Main Street wanted to see the fight. It was clear who the favorite was. Jake may have alienated a lot of people in town with his journalism, but J.J. was probably the most hated man in the county. Nearly everyone wanted to see Jake break the big man in half.

Jake tried to clear his head, and in doing so let J.J. in too close. J.J. tried to bear hug Jake, and out of desperation Jake gave J.J. a series of body punches to the kidneys. J.J. loosened his grip, and Jake stepped inside low and continued to punch to J.J.'s body.

People remarked at how poorly J.J. defended himself against someone who was motivated and had a few skills. Jake was not a small man, but it was his determination that carried him through. He stepped back and tried to make J.J. mad again. This tactic turned out to be his best weapon.

"What's the matter big mouth?" Jake taunted. "Got your dress on today?"

J.J. was like a raging elephant. Now he went berserk. Nobody talked to him like that.

Jake might have been over playing this strategy; after-all, J.J. could kill Jake if given half a chance. The trick was to keep him mad, stay on the outside, and keep him off guard with continuous and measured punches, in the hope that J.J. would flail away in his anger.

Jake also knew that he was in much better condition than his opponent, so keeping him at bay was going to wear J.J. down. Jake figured that it was just a matter of time before the big man got tired and opened himself up to a clean punch. The trick was to keep out of J.J.'s reach until that happened. If J.J. ever got a firm grip on Jake, the fight could be over as quickly as it had started.

J.J. came in again swinging wildly. A couple of punches landed, and Jake retreated a little. Encouraged,

J.J. came in again, faster this time, and Jake sidestepped him once more with another punch to the ear. J.J. went down again, this time to the obvious approval of the crowd.

The audience was openly cheering Jake, which seemed to have a negative effect on J.J.'s morale. J.J. stopped briefly to look around the circle of townspeople that had the combatants surrounded. He saw the blood thirst on the faces of some. Looking back at Jake, it now seemed that he was fighting the whole town. His enthusiasm for the fight began to wane, and Jake could sense it.

"We can end it here J.J.," Jake said breathing deeply. "If you walk away now, you can save a little face. But if I can whip you in front of all of these people, you are finished in this town."

"You will never whip me Jake."

This time Jake was the aggressor. J.J. had been a little distracted as he looked at the crowd. Seeing this, Jake kept him talking while he maneuvered himself closer. Jake decided it was now or never. He was going to let it all out.

Jake stepped in close suddenly, the big man gasping for air, and hit him low in the stomach. J.J. doubled over briefly and groaned but came up and landed a straight left on Jake's chin.

But the big man's punches had lost a lot of steam, and although his punch straightened Jake up a little, he came right back into a slightly crouching position and continued to punch the big man in the abdomen.

The two men now traded punches for a few seconds, both getting in some good shots, right, left, right, left. But the big man was clearly running out of steam. He had put out a lot more energy. Jake was tiring too, but he was still fresh enough to hurt J.J.

J.J. finally straightened up to give Jake a big over hand right, but Jake beat J.J. to the punch with a strait left, then another, then another, and when J.J. seemed about ready to fall from shear exhaustion, Jake patiently measured his opponent, moved in at just the right moment, leaned his body into the punch, and shot a massive right to the big man's face.

"This one's for Sol," Jake said loud enough for the crown to hear.

J.J.'s head snapped back from the thunderous punch, his eyes rolled into his head, and with his knees buckling from underneath him, he hit the dirt a final time.

The crowd cheered with great enthusiasm and surrounded Jake, patting him on the back and congratulating him. The crowd slowly dispersed, leaving Jake standing over his downed opponent.

Nobody stooped to lend J.J. a hand.

"Quite a display, Jake. I didn't know you had it in you."

Jake managed to focus through the fog in his head to see Gordy standing on the boardwalk with a broad smile on his face.

"Let's get you cleaned up," he said.

"What about him?" Jake said nodding his head toward the downed man.

"He looks like he is still breathing. If he is still there when I get back, I will call a doctor."

The two men laughed.

"Ouch," Jake said through a split lip.

Jake and Gordy entered Barney's. Some of the patrons applauded. Jake felt much better as Barney came to the table with a wet towel.

"That man is a load," Jake said.

"You seemed to be doing all right," Gordy answered.

"Maybe, but it was touch and go there for a while. I am not in a hurry for a re-match."

"Well, you will be happy to know that the Sheriff's Department is investigating the fire, and it looks like we may be able to pin it on J.J. We have a witness who will testify that J.J. was out back of your place minutes before the fire. And from the looks of the fire pattern, there is little doubt it was set. This was no accident."

"Maybe, but his dad will get him off like always," Jake said.

"You may be right. Some things are out of my

control. But if Mr. Osgood doesn't let his son face the music this time, his reputation might suffer. And if he lost credibility in this community, I don't think his ego could take it. Without the adulation of the people here, John Sr. becomes just another schmuck like the rest of us."

"I'd like to see that," Jake said.

"Well, you may. Beating up a migrant worker is one thing, but the community won't stand for J.J. destroying the property of a prominent citizen, especially right in the heart of town. Even his dad is smart enough to realize that. Besides, word has it that his father is getting fed up with his son's antics. There is also talk that Osgood has state level political aspirations. It may be that he lets his son face the music for once for his own good.

"So, what about you, Jake? What now?"

"Well," Jake said, "my equipment is gone, I have no money, and I probably couldn't get a loan anywhere in the county after my editorials on the strike. I guess I am finished."

"Yesterday I would have agreed with you, but there are a lot of people in this community who think an awful lot less of J.J. and his father than they do you. You made a lot of friends today that you may have not realized you had. Public opinion still counts for a lot in Citrus Grove, and there are some people here who know what you did was right."

"Does that include you, Gordy?"

"Yes, including me."

"I think I will be going," Jake said.

"Thanks for the towel," Jake shouted to Barney as he headed for the front door.

Gordy walked his friend to the street.

"I guess I should go and check on J.J. Where are you headed, Jake?"

"I think I will go home to see if there is anything I can salvage."

As Jake walked down the street to his apartment, his ribs hurt, his eye was swollen, and he had a cut on his cheek.

"I feel great," he said to himself.

The inside of his apartment was filled with soot, but his closet was mostly intact. He still had a few clothes, but that was all he ever had.

He gathered up what clothes he could; they smelled of smoke. He put them in a duffle back that had been lying on the floor of the closet and tossed it in front of the door.

Jake figured he wouldn't be back anytime soon, so he stepped to his front window for one more look. It was a great vantage point to the street, and he always enjoyed looking out of it.

He lingered at the window for a few minutes, looking up and down the street as he always had done.

"I've got to get out of here," he finally said out

loud to himself.

His next stop was the Delgado's, where he was offered dinner and an indefinite place to stay.

Mrs. Delgado offered to wash his clothes.

Jake didn't have much to say. He ate dinner in virtual silence as he listened to the normal family banter of his friends. After dinner he excused himself and went to bed.

Jake lay in bed for quite a while. His mind raced. He thought about the last few months. He thought about his options. He thought about his future.

"What the hell am I going to do now?" he thought to himself.

"I might be able to get a job at the Globe. I know a lot of people there. And some of them have been friends of mine for a long time. The problem is that they are all pro-farmer. Some of them were even offended by my editorials. They believe the union was communist. Maybe they would be willing to overlook the last few months, but I wouldn't bet the farm on it."

Jake thought about re-opening his business, but he knew that he would have to revert back to the same kind of journalism he now hated. He didn't want to be the community cheerleader anymore. He was tired of reporting on church socials, service club fundraisers, Fourth of July celebrations and high school sports. Not that he now saw himself as above it all. He appreciated how parents would take pride in seeing their kids written up in the local newspaper. But he wanted to tell all of the news, and if he couldn't tell the whole truth, warts and all, then he didn't want any part of it anymore.

"If not journalism, then what?" he thought. "What else can I do?"

And if the Depression was still on at next year's cotton harvest, which was not really that far off, would he find himself back in the same situation again? His choices on how to cover the news would be the same as before, and he didn't like being thought of as the community pariah.

Sol could come into town, speak his mind, stir up trouble, and leave. The community newspaper man would be left behind to face the community.

And what if Veronica came back this fall? Cotton harvest workers would be returning in about seven months, just around the corner. He loved her. He had decided that much, and if he came out of the closet and openly embraced his ethnicity, he knows he would lose a lot of the support that he had gained today. But, if he didn't openly embrace the truth of his background, he doubted that Veronica would fully respect him even if they did get together. They could never be happy if he doubted her love and respect.

And what about her? Did she feel the same way toward him? Did he want to wait until the end of summer to find out? And what if she didn't still want him? Then what?

He rolled this over and over in his mind until he finally fell asleep.

His sleep was broken when Senor Delgado knocked on his door for breakfast.

Jake ate in silence, and the Delgados left him alone, knowing he needed to think.

Mrs. Delgado had somehow known what was on his mind, because she packed his clothes in an old suitcase that her husband had scrounged out of the attic.

Jake stood on the Delgado front porch with his suitcase in his hand. His host did not ask questions. He knew Jake was in a private place in his mind.

"You know you are always welcome here, my friend," Mr. Delgado said to Jake. "Our door is always open to you."

"Muchas gracias. I am fortunate to have a friend like you."

Jake descended the steps and began walking toward the center of town.

Jake walked down the street with a new sense of optimism. He had decided his future, let the chips fall where they may. Reaching the downtown area, Jake took a seat on the bus bench in front of the Foreign Legion Hall. There was no bus depot in town. Citrus Grove was too small of a community for that. But there was regular bus service up and down the valley between Sacramento and Los Angeles, one northbound bus and one southbound bus every day.

From Sacramento a traveler could change busses to San Francisco in the west and to Salt Lake City and Denver in the east. From LA one could connect to the desert communities of south east California an on to Arizona and New Mexico from there.

Jake sat in the sun, about as happy as anyone could be. His face still hurt, but his spirits were high.

"What are you doing here, Jake?" Gordy asked, appearing seemingly out of nowhere.

"I am waiting for the bus."

"The bus! What in the world for?"

"I am leaving town," Jake replied.

"Leaving town! What about your newspaper business?"

"It wouldn't work, Gordy. You know that. I'd be kidding myself. Besides, I am not the person you think I am. And I am going to find myself."

"I don't know what you are talking about, Jake."

"I know, Gordy. But trust me. It is too hard to explain."

"But where are you going?"

"I am headed to the Imperial Valley."

"Why would you want to go there?"

"There is someone I need to find," Jake said. "I

think she holds the key to my future, and I am going after it."

"Oh, it's like that, someone with the key to your heart, you mean. I might have known it had something to do with a woman. Anyone I know?"

"No, she would not run in the same circles that you do."

"I see. Will you be coming back?"

Jake saw the bus coming down the street.

"I might be back this fall. I haven't decided yet. It depends on what happens in the next few months."

The bus pulled up to the curb as the air breaks shushed. Jake was the only passenger waiting to board. The door opened, and Jake grabbed a hold of the handle next to the door.

"Is there anything I can do for you, Jake?"

"No, Gordy, but thanks."

Jake put a foot on the first step of the bus and stopped, turning his head.

"You know, Gordy. There is one thing you can do for me."

"Name it my friend?"

"The next time you see me, call me Juan."

Jake stepped aboard and found a seat as the bus drove away.

About The Author

Originally from the Boyle Heights district of East Los Angeles, California, Robert Torres earned a Bachelor's Degree in journalism from California State University, Fresno in 1988 and worked his way through graduate school as a news and feature writer for area newspapers.

Torres went on to obtain a Master's Degree in History at CSUF in 1994 and was awarded Honorable Mention for his thesis on the cotton workers strike of 1933, which was the basis for his first book, "San Joaquin Valley Cotton War."

Robert Torres has spent the last twenty five years studying and writing about Mexican-American issues. He has taught California History, Latin American History and Chicano Studies at Bakersfield College and has also served as a visiting lecturer at California State University Bakersfield.